THE
SPECTER

Also by Joan Lowery Nixon:

The Kidnapping of Christina Lattimore
The Séance

THE SPECTER

JOAN LOWERY NIXON

DELACORTE PRESS/NEW YORK

Published by
Delacorte Press
1 Dag Hammarskjold Plaza
New York, N.Y. 10017

Manufactured in the United States of America
First printing

Library of Congress Cataloging in Publication Data

Nixon, Joan Lowery.
The specter.

Summary: A seventeen-year-old orphan with Hodgkin's
disease becomes very involved with her new hospital
roommate, a nine-year-old girl who insists that
the man who killed her father is trying to kill her.
[1. Orphans—Fiction.   2. Hodgkin's disease—Fiction.
3. Emotional problems—Fiction]   I. Title.
PZ7.N65Sp   [Fic]   82-70322
ISBN 0-440-08063-0   AACR2

*To my friend James M. Skelton, Jr., M.D.,
in appreciation of his advice
and encouragement*

CHAPTER

1

The whisper strikes through the darkness, and I struggle to meet it, clutching at the sound.

"Sikes!" It comes again, a terrifying hiss.

Did something in the darkness move? Is something there? I grope for the light cord that dangles over the metal headboard of my hospital bed.

"Who's there?" I stammer, and the sound of my voice in that dark room frightens me even more.

No one answers, but I can feel the tension of someone listening. My fingers jerk the cord, and I swing my feet over the edge of the bed. With the courage that comes only from that rush of light I jump up and throw back the white cotton curtain that separates my bed from that of the child by the window.

Through the guardrail she stares at me with enormous, deep blue eyes in a face that is as pale as her hair. It's the first time she's opened them since she was brought to the hospital this morning. It's as though the whisperer had broken a spell.

We are two scared people confronting each other. Her small body is a rigid board, her hands like white clamps on the edges of the mattress.

"Sikes?" It's a question, and her glance darts about the room.

Her voice is so thin, so terrified, that I put the rail down and sit on the edge of her bed. I grasp her right hand, uncoiling her taut fingers and wrapping them in my own.

"Sikes was here," she says.

"Don't be scared," I tell her. "Look around the room. I'm the only one here."

I can feel her begin to relax, cautiously, a little cat staring out the territory. I sit with her quietly because I don't know what to say.

Mrs. Rosa Cardenas, the round little nurse's aide who gives back rubs the way she'd knead bread, fills me each day with fruit juice and hospital gossip. Through her I know that this little girl, who looks as though she's about nine or ten, had been with her parents in a fiery one-car smashup on I-10, heading toward the hill country out of San Antonio. Her parents had been killed, but she had come out of it with what they hoped was nothing more than a concussion.

I also know that she has been unconscious from the time she was thrown from the car; so I jump when she suddenly says, "Sikes killed my father."

It's creepy. I don't want to handle it. I jab at the button for the night nurse.

"He was here, you know," she says.

I don't know anything. Yes, someone had whispered. But maybe it was this kid. I had first thought someone had been in the room, but I hadn't actually seen anyone. Sikes? Who was Sikes? I hit the button again, wishing the nurse would hurry.

"Don't go away," the girl says. Her fingers cling to mine so tightly it's painful.

"Hey, it's all right," I say. "I'm in the bed next to yours. I'm not going anywhere."

The anger comes back with a rush, and I tuck it around me, hating my body that has brought me to this place.

"Who are you?" the girl asks.

"Dina Harrington," I answer. Then I remember that no one in the hospital knows who she is. They found a wallet with a driver's license with her father's name on it. Out of state, with an address that doesn't exist, according to Mrs. Cardenas.

There was no identification for the mother. Whatever was in the car had burned. Mrs. Cardenas, having a brother-in-law in the police department, is a great source of information.

"You haven't told me your name," I say. I work the call button.

"Julie," she answers. Her eyes never leave my face.

It bothers me that she isn't asking the right questions. I don't expect her to gasp "Where am I?" like in an old movie. But shouldn't she call for her mother? Or try to find out what happened? Is she in some kind of state of shock?

The door flies open, and Mrs. Marsh, the tall nurse with the mole on her chin, comes in. There's a black hair growing out of the mole, and when she talks to me, I go crazy trying not to stare at that mole.

"Mrs. Marsh never smiles," I once told Mrs. Cardenas.

Mrs. Cardenas shrugged. "She has problems."

"Who hasn't?"

"Her husband told her he wanted a bigger house. They sold their old house. She went out looking at model homes, and he took off with the money and the receptionist in his office. *¡El diablo!*"

"She's awake," I tell Mrs. Marsh. "She thinks someone was in the room. She—"

I stop in mid-sentence as Mrs. Marsh briskly and efficiently begins doing all the temperature, pulse, and straightening-up things that nurses do, seemingly ignoring me. She shoos me out of the way.

"Get back in bed, Dina," she says. "Leave the light on, please. The doctor on duty will be here in a few minutes." She yanks the curtain back into place between our two beds and leaves the room.

The door swings shut without a sound, but Julie's voice is like a shiver behind that over-laundered barricade.

"I don't want to be alone," she whimpers. "Could you pull back the curtains?"

"Sure." I manage it with one swift sweep of my arm.

This time it's my own bed I sit on, dangling my legs over the side.

"Don't go away," Julie tells me.

"I'm here," I say. "I'll be here a long time after you've gone home with your relatives."

"I haven't got any."

It dawns on me that she knows her mother is dead, too. I shudder. "Don't you have a grandmother? An aunt? Somebody?"

"No."

We've got something in common, although I've had seventeen years to get used to it.

The door opens, and I quickly swing my legs up on the bed and pull the blanket up to my chin, covering my clumsy cotton gown. A stocky man with bristling yellow hair strides into the room. He's wearing the traditional white coat, but green plaid slacks stick out at the bottom like two grass-hopper legs. Mrs. Cardenas says that Dr. Paull is going to be a good doctor someday, when he starts liking his patients; but for now he's my least favorite person around the hospital.

Mrs. Marsh, who has followed him, moves be-

tween the beds and reaches out for the curtain. But
Julie cries out, "No! Don't do that! I want Dina
to be here. If she's here, Sikes won't come back."

"Who is Sikes?" the doctor asks. He puts up a
hand to stop the nurse.

"He killed my father," Julie says.

The doctor is silent for a moment, studying her.
"You know about the accident?"

His glance moves to me, and I shrug. "I didn't
tell her. She told me."

"I was supposed to be killed, too," Julie says
without emotion, as though she is talking about
someone who doesn't exist.

Dr. Paull ignores this, and I wonder why. Maybe
he thinks Julie is out of her head. Shouldn't he ask
her about it?

"We've checked you carefully," he says. "For-
tunately, we think you've had nothing more than
a concussion, but now that you're conscious, we'll
be able to make some more tests."

That's a dumb way to talk to a little kid. I have
my mouth open to translate, but he goes on.

"Does your head hurt?"

"Yes."

He sits on the edge of her bed. He is close enough
to me so that I can smell his woodsy shaving lotion
and see a little wrinkle flicker between his eyebrows
as he talks. He pushes back the sleeve of Julie's hospital gown and studies the bruises on her arm.

I study them, too. Anyone can see they aren't
from the accident. They are old, browning bruises,

and I wonder how she got them. I want to ask, but decide I had better keep my mouth shut. Dr. Paull shines a light into Julie's eyes and makes a satisfied hum-humming noise.

Finally he takes a slow breath. "We don't know your first name," he tells her.

"Julie."

"How old are you, Julie?"

"Nine."

"And where do you live? Can you give us an address?"

"No," she says. "We just lived in San Antonio a week. It was an apartment house. It's next to the freeway."

"How about a former address? Where did you live before?"

"Lots of places. We used to live in a mobile home. We moved a lot." She is staring at him, and his wrinkle flickers like a bad light bulb.

"It would help us if we could find your relatives. Can you give us some names and addresses?"

"I haven't got any relatives," she tells him.

Dr. Paull smooths down her sleeve and gently pats her hand. Maybe Mrs. Cardenas is right about him.

"We don't know much about you, Julie," he says. "Can you talk to us about what happened?"

She doesn't move. I don't see her even blink.

"You and your parents were traveling in a car, Julie. You were in the backseat, apparently. We're guessing, from the police report, that there was some malfunction in the car, that your father in some way lost control of the car."

"Sikes killed my father."

How can she say this in such a calm way? I shiver again.

"Julie," Dr. Paull says quietly, "your father was killed in the accident. Your mother was killed, too. Can you tell us her name?"

"Nancy." Tears begin to roll from her eyes as she continues to gaze into his face.

I hug my knees with a sense of relief. Tears I can understand. But there is so much I don't understand, including myself. I wish I could leave this place, with its smells of laundry-soaped sheets and alcohol rubs. Even leave my body, moving out and away, through the walls, through the air like so much vanishing mist, and never come back.

Dr. Paull takes a clipboard from the nurse and scratches at the paper with an old pocket pen. "We're going to give you medication to help take away your headache, Julie," he says. He stands and pats her hand again before gently placing it on the bed.

Mrs. Marsh makes quick movements with a hypo and a bottle; rolls Julie onto her side, pulling back the bedcovers; and zaps a needle into her hip. I wince, but Julie doesn't seem to notice what is happening.

She slowly closes her eyes. Her shoulders relax, and she sinks a little deeper into the bed. Mrs. Marsh slams the protective rail back into place.

The doctor turns and looks at me. He leafs through some papers, finally looks up, and says, "Dina Harrington." That's all.

I had almost begun to like this man when I saw him pat Julie's hand. But now I'm angry at him. I didn't used to get so angry at people. Dr. Lynn Manning, the resident psychiatrist, tells me I'm really angry at myself. I try to remember this. It's not Dr. Paull's fault that I'm here. But it is partly his fault that I don't like to be here.

"Shouldn't something go with the Dina Harrington?" I ask him. "Like, 'How are you feeling?' or 'Any more problems with nausea?'"

"According to what I read on the chart, you're progressing satisfactorily."

"Not me. The chart." I try to sound matter-of-fact, but it's hard to keep the anger out of my voice. "The chart is progressing satisfactorily, but I'm going to die. Didn't the chart tell you that?"

Mrs. Marsh sniffs and looks upward, as though to say, "She's being a problem." The hair in her mole quivers, and I have to wrench my gaze away from it.

Dr. Paull nods and says, "Having a negative attitude won't help you."

"Nothing is going to help me," I answer. "I'd be stupid not to face the facts."

"Dina, I'm not your doctor," he says. "I'm not going to go into that with you. What I'd like to do is find out if Julie Kaines gave you any information about her family or herself."

I glance over at Julie. She's asleep and breathing

smoothly, her straggly blond hair tangled around her thin face. "She talked about this person Sikes. She thought he was in the room."

"Aside from that nightmare," he says.

"Why do you think it was just a nightmare?" I ask him. "I heard the whisper, too. It might have been Julie. It might have been someone else. It felt as though someone was in the room. It was dark in here, and I was scared."

The wrinkle between his eyebrows is at it again. "You didn't see anyone?"

"It could be I didn't see anyone because it was dark and because it took a while to turn on the light. If someone was here, he'd have had time to get out of the room."

"You think someone was in the room?"

"Yes." I sigh. "Oh, I don't know."

"Did Julie talk about what happened? About any relatives who might come for her?"

"She said she didn't have any relatives."

"No one? That's hard to believe."

"Believe it. I'm proof that it's possible."

He looks embarrassed. That's a step in the right direction. But he turns away from me and talks to Mrs. Marsh. "Maybe the patient will be more communicative in the morning."

"She's not a patient. She's a person!" I say. "And she's scared. Can't you see that she's scared of this guy Sikes? She said he killed her father."

"Her mother and father were killed this morning in an automobile accident."

"But what if Sikes tampered with the car? I saw that once in a movie on television. The brake line was cut, and the car went out of control. Couldn't that have happened?"

"It's up to the police to investigate things like that," he says. "What we need to find out is who can take responsibility for Julie."

As he walks toward the door, he pauses. "If she talks to you tomorrow, Dina, and tells you about any relatives or friends, please let one of the nurses know."

For the first time he smiles at me. Maybe he's trying to be friendly. Maybe he's just wanting me to do things his way. Maybe he's remembering what he learned in medical school about how to be nice to patients—if they teach anything like that.

I don't want to sort it out. I just wiggle down under the blanket and sheet and pull them up around my ears, curling into a ball. I snake one hand out and pull the string attached to the light chain, snapping the room into darkness. I squeeze my eyes shut and listen to them leave.

I'm not going to make any promises to him. Julie's life is her own, not mine. What she wants to tell people is up to her.

The anger I feel toward the doctor and the nurse, the anger for being pushed into someone else's life, meets my old, familiar anger head-on, leaving me uncomfortable and confused.

And so I retreat. I have learned to move out and away from the pain and the illness, becoming a separate being from my body. I pull away from these feelings now, away from my body, away from the hospital room; and my mind slips through the moonlit rooms of the place where I grew up, the church-run foster home for girls like me, whose absent parents clung legally until their children were unadoptable. People want babies to adopt, they told me over and over, as I wrapped gangly legs around chair rungs and ached to be small and petted and loved.

Now I am far from my body, and I glide through the living room of the central building, stroking the smooth oak tabletops and the sturdy upholstered chairs. I had once thought them ugly, and they were. They are. But they are an anchor to my other world, and I need to touch them.

The moon shimmers through windows without drapes, open to the fields and the woods of gnarled elm and mesquite, and I can see beyond to the vegetable garden where I once helped to hoe fat clumps of weeds from between rows of pole beans and corn, whacking the weed roots with a vengeance in the hot summer sun, clods of dark soil flying into the air, sweat running down my face and back.

Softly, I am now in the kitchen, slipping into one of the wooden chairs, remembering old Carlotta, who does the baking and who hands out cookies like love tokens. Even in the aloneness of night the kitchen is memory-fragrant with cinnamon and chocolate and the warm breasts of Carlotta, who knows when a child needs a hug in order to survive.

And here is the room in which I cried at night when I was very young, wishing someone would want me, wondering how anyone would find me in this hill country place. Here I grew older, no longer caring about the childhood I had once wanted, focusing all my energies on a future I would build for myself.

Holley Jo, my best friend, has been at the home almost as long as I have, and our lives are so intertwined that we would sit cross-legged on our beds after lights out and talk about the years we would plan and how great they would be, until someone would come in from the next room and threaten us with all sorts of dire things unless we let them get to sleep.

As I move through the closed doorway, I am no more opaque than the moonlight that spills over the windowsill. The room is vibrant with rhythmic breathing and sleep murmurs and tiny night noises. Holley Jo's long, brown hair is spidery across the pillow, and I finger it wistfully, thinking of the short, thin curls that are all I have left of the dark hair that once whipped through the air as I ran.

Holley Jo stirs, and I pull my hand away. Hush. Sleep. I'm not here to disturb. I'm here because I'm clinging to something it's hard to give up. My bed is still empty, and I curl up at the end, my cheek against the fuzzy chenille spread. For so many years this bed has been my refuge, my planning place. Here is where I had decided that the whole world ahead was open to me, and what I wanted to work for could be mine. I would aim for a scholarship, and knew I had a darned good chance of getting one. I would go to the University of Texas, and work part time, and live in a dorm, and come out clutching a degree in economics and an acceptance to law school. That's when my real life would begin. I was going to win. I could be patient with the promise of what my life was going to be.

Then that dream was ripped apart and smashed. When the doctor sent me to the hospital in San Antonio and they told me there that the chills and weight loss and that stupid lump on the side of my neck meant Hodgkin's disease, I cried out that it wasn't fair! I couldn't be a winner because they had snatched away the race. And I wasn't ready to die.

"What am I doing here?" I whisper.

Jarringly I am back in the hospital room with its medicine smells and the brisk footsteps following the jangle of a cart in the hallway past my door. The words I had whispered hang in the air, reminding me of another whisper, and I shiver, clutching the blanket to my chin for comfort.

Who are you, Sikes?

Lying there in the dark room, I hold my breath, terrified that I will hear an answer.

CHAPTER

2

Hospital mornings break the day into clatters and rattles with a background of voices, even before the sun is up. There's not much privacy in a hospital. We can't keep from hearing what goes on in the rooms around us.

There's an old lady across the hall who sometimes cries like a little kid and keeps calling, "Eddie! Eddie!" Mrs. Cardenas said the old lady is ninety-six, and she wants Eddie to come and take her home, except there isn't an Eddie anymore.

One night I sneaked across the hall and sat in the chair by her bed. I thought if she had someone to talk to, she might feel better. She was like a little skeleton, with transparent skin stretched over her bones; and her fingers kept poking out the top of the blanket, wiggling like spider legs. She stopped crying and stared at me, but she didn't talk; so I told her about Rob, whose tortoiseshell glasses match his hair and slip down his nose when he leans over to write, and about the terrific poetry he writes in English class, and about the special poems he wrote just for me. I told her he had promised to give me his senior ring next year, but since I came to the hospital, I haven't heard from him.

And I told her about the place I lived before I came here, and how my friend, Holley Jo, keeps sending me get-well letters that make me homesick for the low hills and the brown grass in the fall and the wild flowers in the spring, and even for the dust smell of the garden and the rattling bus to school.

And I told her they said I couldn't go back there to live again because they had no facilities for taking the right kind of care of me. And I told her I was going to die.

She just kept staring at me, and all of a sudden she made noises and began to smell awful. So I ran back to my own bed and scrunched down under the blanket and cried.

This morning—the day after Julie had come— is just like every other morning, with all the bustle of trays and face washings that have to take place before anyone is really awake. My doctor won't come by until ten, so there's going to be a long wait after the breakfast trays are picked up. I take a shower, then decide to paint my toenails. Holley

Jo sent me the nail polish in my favorite shade of pink.

I glance over at Julie. "You didn't eat much breakfast."

"I don't like that stuff," she answers.

I can see they've given her a liquid diet. They probably have to until they find out if everything is all right.

My knee is tucked under my chin, and I take a smooth stroke with the brush, thinking at the same time how pale and spindly my legs look. I need the sun.

"That's pretty," Julie says.

I hold out my foot, stretching my toes, and smile at her. "Would you like me to paint your toenails, too?"

She nods, so I pull the sheet and blanket away from the end of the bed, put her feet on my lap, and paint away.

I am just finishing when a nurse's aide comes in and watches us, shaking her head. "She's not supposed to move around," she tells me.

"Only her feet got moved," I answer, "and the concussion isn't in her toes."

Julie actually smiles, and she lifts her feet to examine her toes. It's funny how a little thing like nail polish can make you feel better about yourself—even if the feeling lasts for only a few moments.

"Julie, I've brought you a comb and hair brush and toothpaste and the other things you'll need," the aide says. She pulls the curtain between our beds and tells me to scoot. Julie's got to have one of those chilly bed baths that make you feel like dried soap for hours.

"Don't go away," Julie tells me.

"I'm right here," I say. I turn on the television, and sit on my bed cross-legged, brushing my hair. In all my jumbled-up memories of what happened to me after I came to this hospital, one of the worst was losing my hair. I was sick—so terribly sick—from the radiation and the medication they were giving me, and I was weak and sore and tired from the bone marrow tests and the operation. For a while pain was not just a word. It was a monster that had come to inhabit my body.

"What is a spleen, anyway?" I had asked.

They said it wasn't important to me, and I'd never miss it, and it had to come out. And after they studied it and tested it, they said encouraging things. But my mind did not agree they told the truth, because my miserable body was the lie.

On my back, in bed, I'd watch the little cracks in the plaster near the ceiling, watch them come together like a tiny face with fat cheeks and puckered lips. And I'd drift in and out of the pain and the illness and think about what mattered most— my hair.

When I began to feel better, someone gave me a wig. It made me look as though I had just stepped out of a beauty parlor some time in the sixties. It was made of washable stuff and had a permanent curl. Oh, how I missed my own hair!

What was growing on my head now was soft and curly and baby-fine, and I had the weird feeling that I'd been given the wrong hair.

Holley Jo and I used to measure our hair with a tape measure to see whose was the longest, and we'd brush our hair each night, feeling it slither down over our shoulders.

I wasn't going to wear it that long forever. The day I graduated from college I planned to have it cut in one of those smart, straight hairstyles that would be just right for a woman with a degree in economics who was on her way to law school.

"Why are you thinking of economics, Dina?" Mrs. Schaefer, the math teacher, had asked me.

I rested my elbows on her desk, leaning into her smile. "Because I like the way economics puts everything into order. Because the laws of economics make A lead to B, and it's fair. I like things to be fair," I added.

Fair? I found out that nothing is fair.

"I didn't know they had televisions in hospitals." The voice sounds a little stronger.

I climb off the bed and poke my head around the curtain. The nurse's aide has left, and I haven't even noticed.

"The board of directors at the home where I live paid for it."

"What are you watching?"

"I have no idea." I really haven't noticed. It's a game show, and it runs into the next game show, which runs into the next day, I guess. They all look alike.

"Can you pull the curtain back?" Julie asks.

"Sure," I say, and proceed to do so.

"The nurse this morning was nice," Julie says.

"Some of the people around here are real nice," I tell her. "Wait until you meet Mrs. Cardenas. She gives back rubs and she's full of good stories."

"I'm going to have some X rays this morning," Julie says. "They're going to wheel me down to the X-ray room on a cart. The nurse told me. She said it won't hurt, and I shouldn't be afraid."

But fear is in her eyes. I sit on the edge of her bed again. "X rays are just a way of taking pictures. They aren't anything for you to be scared of."

"I wish you could come with me."

"They'd never let me. But remember—I told you I'll be here when you come back."

"Promise?" Julie says, and I wonder where they'll send her to live.

"Promise," I answer.

"I'll try not to be scared."

I look at her thin arms, bare against the white sheets, each discolored bruise standing out.

"You're afraid of a lot of things, aren't you?" I ask. When she doesn't answer, I add, "You can't keep all that fear inside. I think you should talk to someone who could help. Maybe the police."

For a moment she grows even more pale. She

grips my hand, and I'm startled at how strong she is. "No!"

"Okay," I say. "But you're awfully scared of that guy Sikes. You said last night that he killed your father, and that you were supposed to die. If I thought someone was going to try to murder me, I'd yell for help."

Her fingernails are digging into my hand. "You help me," she says.

"I can't help you the way the police could."

I shift on the bed and try to pry her fingers loose. She's stronger than I am and she's hurting me.

"Stay here," she says. "I need you to be here."

"Okay, but stop hurting my hand."

She looks surprised, and I can see her trying to relax.

"Thanks," I say, and rub my hand. "You want me to help you. Are you going to talk to me?"

Her eyes narrow just a little. "About what?"

"For one thing, about how the people at the hospital can contact your relatives."

"I haven't got any. Really."

"How about where you were living before you moved to San Antonio? Aren't there any friends of the family?"

Her face puckers up like one of those dolls made out of dried apples, and she starts to cry. "We moved and moved and moved! And I don't have anybody!"

Awkwardly I smooth back her hair, trying not

to feel guilty for causing the tears. "Hey, Julie, it's okay. Don't cry," I say.

Julie suddenly pulls up and flings herself at me, hanging on as though we're in the middle of Canyon Lake and I'm the only life preserver.

"I want to stay with you," she says.

"Julie, I can't take care of you. I can't even take care of myself."

Her body is shaking now, and I try to move her back on the bed, to help her lie down, but she won't budge. "Please," she sobs.

Warm tears are dripping down my neck, and I squirm away from them, saying, "Look, I'll see what I can do. Okay? Please stop crying."

It helps a bit, but a nurse comes in, gets excited, and sends me back to bed.

"I don't know what happened," I tell her. "I guess I said the wrong thing."

"She shouldn't be upset," the nurse tells me. She soothes Julie and wipes her nose and washes her face again.

I lie in bed watching some fat woman on the television screen jump up and down and beat on the master of ceremonies, and I wonder if she'll have a heart attack with all that screaming. And I wonder what made Julie cry with so much desperation.

Were some of those tears for her mother and father? I've never seen anyone so panicked before, and it seems to me that it takes more than one problem to make someone explode like that. I can't figure out why she doesn't want to tell the police about Sikes if she's afraid she's going to be murdered. It doesn't make sense.

The door bursts open, and a pair of orderlies fasten it against the wall. They rattle the cart to the side of Julie's bed and lift her onto it. As they wheel her out of the room, she holds out a hand toward me. Her eyes are pleading.

"I'll be here when you get back, Julie," I tell her.

They release the door, but it does a double flutter as Dr. Hector Cruz comes in, stepping out of the way of the cart. He's a quiet man, with not much hair on top and a nose that looks as though it had been in a lot of rough football games. He perches stoop-shouldered on the side of my bed and smiles at me.

"I know better than to ask how you're feeling," he says. "Last time I asked, your answer went on for five minutes."

"I'm sorry," I say. "Sometimes I get angry."

"There's nothing wrong with being angry. It's a human emotion. It's what you do with the anger that counts."

"Sometimes feeling angry is the only thing that helps," I answer. But at the same time I remember Dr. Lynn telling me how people can cling to their anger because they're afraid to leave it and take the next step.

"Let's talk about remission," he says in his calm way. "I don't think you really understand it."

I stuff a pillow against the painted headboard of the bed and wedge myself against it, pulling my knees up under the bedspread and wrapping my arms around them.

Dr. Cruz waits until I've settled down and says, "If you understand remission, you might feel better about what is happening to you. You've responded very well to treatment, and we feel your disease is in remission. That means during a certain period the disease will not progress. How long the period will last we can't say, but we have hopes it will be for a number of years."

"And after that? We're back to zero. Right?"

"We're back to more treatment, and a hopeful chance for another remission." He takes my hand and looks at me earnestly. "Dina, the scientists who are working so hard to discover a cure might—"

I interrupt. "They've been working to find a cure for cancer for a hundred years!"

"There are many forms of cancer. Hodgkin's disease has its own characteristics, and there has been great progress made in moving toward a cure. There are many people living active lives with the disease in remission, who wouldn't have been able to do so years ago."

"You sound like a textbook."

"I'm offering you the facts."

"You're offering me wishful thinking."

"I'm offering you hope."

"Same thing."

He sits there rubbing his chin. Finally he says, "Doctors have found that a patient's attitude can mean a great deal of difference in whether he's cured or whether he dies from a serious disease."

Another woman is screaming on the television. Another winner. Mornings full, days full, weeks full of winners. Who cares? I snap the off button and blot her out as though she never existed.

"Please don't talk to me about my attitude, Dr. Cruz." I try to keep my voice quiet and calm to match his. "I had a whole life ahead of me, filled with all the things I wanted—a career and love and all I was going to be and do. And you're holding out scraps of it, little pieces that won't add up to anything. How can you expect me to be happy about that?"

"I didn't say 'happy.' I want you to simply make the most of the life you do have."

I close my eyes and shake my head. "Let's not talk about it anymore."

"All right," he says. "Let's talk about your leaving the hospital."

For a moment I can't breathe. My eyelids snap open. "You mean I can go back?"

"No," he says. "You need to live here in San Antonio, where you can be treated at the hospital as an outpatient."

"But where? I don't know anyone here."

He smiles again. "Oh, little Dina, do you think we'd turn you out with a map and an apartment guide? Believe me, we'll find a foster family who'll take good care of you."

I realize I'm not thinking clearly. I'm trying to absorb this news. I'm surprised to find that I dread having to live with strangers. I long for the comfort of the home that's familiar to me, the people I know.

And there was a promise.

"What about the little girl they put in this room —the one who was in the accident—Julie Kaines? What are they going to do about her?"

"I don't know," he says. "She isn't my patient."

I lean forward and grab his arm. "Listen, Dr. Cruz, she's awfully frightened. She hasn't got any relatives and doesn't even want to talk about where she's lived. I think she's afraid to tell anyone— even me. But she does trust me, and she made me promise I'd stay with her. I can't break that promise."

"You can't stay here," he says. "You're well enough to leave the hospital as soon as they find a home for you."

"I guess what I mean is, could they put both of us in the same home? At least for a few months? I think it would help her if we stayed together for a while."

He studies me for a moment. Then he says, "I'd have to talk to her doctor, of course, and I don't know how all the red tape works. I'll ask a few questions. We'll see what we can find out."

I know what he's thinking. He's wondering if this will help me get my mind going in the direction he wants. I'll let him jump to any conclusions he wants. I won't tell him that it's not going to do me a bit of good.

It's just that I made a promise to Julie. And I can understand how scared she is. I've been scared, too. What I don't understand is why no one around here seems to be worried about what Julie said—that she was supposed to die, too. I can't walk away and leave her with a fear that she might be murdered. Just because no one saw that guy Sikes doesn't mean he wasn't in the room.

Dr. Cruz picks up his clipboard and makes some notes. Then he gives me another big smile. I automatically smile back, and he looks pleased and encouraged.

"I'll try," he says again, and leaves the room.

A hospital volunteer comes by with the mail, and I reach for my letter, hoping it's from Holley Jo, who hasn't written for almost two weeks. Or Rob. Just once, if it could be from Rob. But it's never been from Rob. I open a funny card from Carlotta, just signed with her name.

The morning sunlight hurts my eyes, making them water, and I blink. I'm glad she sent me the card, but couldn't she tell me what was happening at the home? Couldn't anyone write that the six-year-olds had started their swimming lessons and they wanted me to come back and be their teacher, or that whoever had replaced me in the first-aid class wishes I was still there?

Couldn't someone say how cool the lake water is early in the morning before the sun has warmed it?

And if the old, blue station wagon still makes that *buckety-buckety* noise that the mechanic never has been able to fix? And if the driver's-ed teacher still keeps teasing the kids in his class, telling the slow, scared ones that they ought to drive in the Indy 500? And if the red clover has faded and the long grass smells dusty-sour in the noon sun?

I'm startled when the door bangs open again and Julie's cart is wheeled through. Her doctor is following. He's a long, thin man whose body dangles through his clothes. He waits until Julie is tucked into bed, and he tries to talk to her; but she gives him the same answers she gives everyone else.

Finally he leaves. Lunches are brought in and slapped on the rolling tables that fit over the beds. Julie's bed is rolled up this time, but she stares at the tray without moving.

"Hey, it's like a big surprise," I tell her. "You take off those metal lids to find out what's underneath." I hop out of bed and pull the covers from the plates. It's an improvement over breakfast, which is a good sign they think she's basically okay.

"How about that! Red Jell-O!" I try to sound enthusiastic. "Everybody likes red Jell-O. Right?"

Julie picks up a spoon. "I like Jell-O. But what's that stuff?"

"Broccoli. Haven't you ever eaten broccoli?"

She shakes her head.

"Well, try some. I think you'll like it."

"No."

"You can't just eat the Jell-O," I tell her. "You have to eat the chicken and the broccoli and the lettuce salad because it's good for you."

I sound like a mother, and I cringe. What am I doing, taking on this little kid?

She obediently takes a mouthful of broccoli, and I climb back in my own bed and eat my lunch before it gets any colder than it was when it was brought in.

Maybe now is a good time to tell her. So I talk about what my doctor said about leaving the hospital, and what I said to him.

She studies me carefully. I can feel her tension.

"It's going to work out all right, Julie," I say. "My doctor's a good guy, and he'll really try to get us a home together."

"When?"

"I don't know. It depends on who they can find. Someone has to want us."

I flip on the television again. I can see Julie trying to keep her eyes open. When the orderly comes in to pick up the trays, I point to Julie's bed, and he slowly rolls it down again.

In a few moments she's asleep. Mrs. Cardenas sticks her head in the door, looks at us both and winks at me. "*Pssst,*" she says, crooking her finger.

I put on my robe and join her in the hall. She's going to retire soon because she says being on her feet so long makes her back hurt. I'm going to miss her.

"I'll walk with you," she says.

"I've been strong enough for a while to walk by myself," I tell her, surprised that she doesn't remember.

"I know," she answers, and she looks both ways before she continues in a conspiratorial voice. "But I got some news about that little girl. The police checked on the driver's license. They found out that William Kaines served time eight years ago in Illinois for assault and rape."

I stop walking and stare at her. "That's awful!"

"For the last few years there wasn't anything on him, and there was nothing left in the car because it burned."

Mrs. Cardenas squeezes my elbow and pilots me down the hallway again. "They may have been the kind who keep one step ahead of the people they owe money to."

It makes me think. "Or ahead of someone who is after them," I say. I look at Mrs. Cardenas, whose round cheeks are red with the excitement of the story she's telling me. "Where did you get this information?"

She begins to look huffy, so I quickly say, "I mean, did the information come from newspapers or the radio news or where?"

She chuckles, her good disposition restored. "Straight from my brother-in-law, Arturo."

"The policeman."

"He ought to know what he's talking about."

"Then, listen. Could he find out something for

me?" I glance down the hall, and one of the nurses is staring at us, head cocked like a banty hen. I grab Mrs. Cardenas's arm and say, "Come on. Keep walking."

She does, leaning close to me. "Find out what?" she asks.

"Could your brother-in-law find out the name of the woman who William Kaines had raped? Could you find out if her last name was Sikes?"

Mrs. Cardenas falters, her mouth a rosy O. "I heard about that Sikes name," she says. "Lorena said the girl had a nightmare last night and that you gave Dr. Paull a bad time."

"Maybe it wasn't just a nightmare. Julie insisted that someone named Sikes was in the room."

"Did you see him? You were in the room, too."

"No. I didn't see him. But I felt someone was there. It was weird."

Her forehead wrinkles up like a pleated collar. "But nobody was in the hospital who shouldn't have been."

I shrug. There's no use arguing. Just because they didn't see anyone leave the room, they don't believe Julie. They didn't see me sneak into the old lady's room either. Not seeing something doesn't mean it didn't happen. After what Mrs. Cardenas has told me, I'm beginning to guess why Julie is so terrified of the man Sikes.

"Well? Can you find out the information I want?"

"Why not?" Mrs. Cardenas says, smiling. "I can usually find out anything."

We've reached the end of the hall and have doubled back, and I haven't noticed. We're close to my room when a scream smashes the air. Someone bursts out of the storeroom and dashes through the door to the stairway. A nurse flaps out of the storeroom screeching that a man had been hiding in there. People begin running toward the stairs and into each other.

I flatten against the wall, pulling Mrs. Cardenas next to me. "Did you get a good look at him?"

"No!" she says. She tugs me toward the nurses' station. We can hear one of the nurses on the phone.

"How should I know?" she's saying. "He was probably looking for drugs, like that creep on the second floor last month."

We hang around, scooping up little pieces of information, until we find that whoever it was has got away, and there are no witnesses—including the nurse who had surprised him in the storeroom, because he had thrown a pillowcase over her head before he shoved past her and ran from the room.

I tell them I think he was tall and had on a blue shirt and pants. The nurse at the desk says she's sure he was wearing dark brown slacks. An orderly who nearly collided with him on the stairs didn't see his face but insists he saw navy blue slacks and a plaid shirt.

"The world is full of strange people," Mrs.

Cardenas says to me. "You go back to your bed for a nap, and I'll call my cousin Carmen, who will want to know all about this."

So I go back into the room. But I stop at the door when I see Julie. She's sitting in the middle of her bed, shaking as though she's naked in a snowstorm.

"Did you see him?" she gasps. "Was it Sikes?"

CHAPTER

3

"No," I say, "it couldn't have been Sikes." And I wonder if I'm lying as I try to soothe away her chattering fear. I know fear. I've watched it flicker behind the tears of kids new to the home in those first days, in which all they knew was that they weren't in control of their lives any longer.

And I knew the gasping, throat-scratching fear that came when my body confirmed what the doctors had told me—the retching, aching fear that lasted until it turned into anger.

"The man in the storeroom was some pot head after drugs," I tell Julie. "Forget him."

She leans back and stares at me with eyes that are cold. "Are you telling me the truth?"

"No one saw him. It all happened too fast."

"Sikes is a murderer," she says. "He killed my father."

I can't go this route again, so I try to change her direction. "Tell me about your father."

Her eyes become softer, and her thin, little face picks up a glow. "My father was tall. He called himself a beanpole. He'd put me on his shoulders and run, and I'd bounce up and down and we'd laugh and laugh. I'd hang onto his chin, but it was prickly. Once my father grew a beard, but it was so light my mother said he looked like a blond Santa Claus, so he shaved it off."

"Did he have the same color hair as you?"

"Yes, and blue eyes, too." She pauses. "Every time my mother said we looked alike, my father would laugh and say, 'How can you think that, Nancy, when Julie is short and doesn't have muscles?' "

She's looking back into another space, and I'm with her, visualizing this tall, young father with the pale hair who looked at the world through eyes like Julie's eyes.

Then I ask the wrong thing. "Julie, how did you get the bruises on your arms?"

She closes up like the petals of a flower in time-lapse photography, shutting me out. A wall of tears, ready to spill, is between us.

"I want to watch television," she says.

I climb on my bed, turning on the controls. It's the afternoon movie, something left over from the forties. Two people have just met at a party and are nose to nose, gulping each other with their eyes. Instant love.

I had liked being in love and in love and in love with some of the boys at school, especially with Rob. The feeling I had for him was a step beyond the early, giggly romances at sweaty school dances with guys with damp hands and the kisses behind the gym before the bus came to take some of us back to the home. Rob had a creative mind, and he gave me copies of the poems he wrote, which I'd read to Holley Jo.

Holley Jo. I think about the way we whispered about our dates after we'd finally settle down to sleep. Sooner or later we'd drowsily slide into our own private daydreams before the night dreams took over, because we knew that someday we'd be women and get beyond the boys to the men, and the love would be for real. Someday.

The familiar exhaustion creeps through me, and I give in to it, unable as ever to fight it. Sleep is a healer, they told me; but sleep is also a private place to hide when thoughts become too hard to handle.

I awake to hear voices. Dr. Lynn Manning is sitting next to Julie's bed. She doesn't look the way a psychiatrist ought to look. I guess I've been influenced by those solemn, bearded pictures of Dr. Sigmund Freud. Dr. Lynn has lots of freckles and a snub nose and reddish hair that curls in every direction. When she smiles, she means it. And when

I talk to her, she really listens. In spite of that white coat, sometimes I forget that she's a doctor.

If anyone can get through to Julie, it will be Dr. Lynn. I'm so glad she's here talking with Julie that I lie on my side and listen in. Dr. Lynn doesn't seem to mind.

But Julie is holding back. These are the same shut-out answers she has given the other doctors. Dr. Lynn gets up and stands at the window, looking out. I've been at that window so many times I can see the scene as though I'm standing with her.

The hospital is built on a hill at the west edge of San Antonio in the medical center. Beyond it are sloping hills that roll one into another, and in the springtime the grass is long and green and shivers in the wind. The hill country stretches out to meet that flat, bright Texas sky, dotted with white globs of clouds that look as though an amateur painter had slapped them there. It's a beautiful country, the only country I've ever known.

"Tell me about your mother," Dr. Lynn says. "What did she like to do?"

Surprisingly Julie responds. "She could sing and dance. She told me she used to work in a nightclub. A long time ago she was in a play."

"A long time ago?"

"When I was little. My father took me to watch, only it was at night, and I fell asleep. So the next morning my mother put on her costume and put me in the big chair in the living room and sang 'As Long As He Needs Me.' She sang it just to me."

Dr. Lynn gives Julie that warm, supportive smile. "Was she in other plays?"

"Maybe before that one," Julie says. "But that was the last."

"Do you know why?"

"No." Her voice becomes tight.

Dr. Lynn sits on the chair by Julie's bed and takes her hand. "It's all right to miss your mother and father. It's all right to cry."

Julie's voice is not much more than a whisper. "I cried for my father. It didn't help. It didn't bring him back."

I can't stand it. There's something she has to tell Dr. Lynn. "Julie," I interrupt. "Tell her about that man you're afraid of."

But Dr. Lynn shakes her head at me. "We'll let Julie take this at her own pace," she says. "Is there anything else you'd like to talk about, Julie?"

"No," Julie says. She slithers down in her bed and pulls the blanket up under her chin.

"All right." Dr. Lynn smiles at her again and moves toward the door. Then she pauses, picks up my robe, which I've left on the end of my bed, and tosses it to me. "Want to go for a walk, Dina?" she asks me.

I really don't, but I climb out of bed, fumble for my slippers, and put on the robe. "Can we walk just as far as the waiting room? I'm tired again."

She puts an arm around my shoulders. "Dr. Cruz tells me that you'll gradually get back much of your energy. He's enthusiastic about your progress."

Before I go through the door, I turn to look at Julie. She's watching me intently. "I'll be back soon," I explain.

Dr. Lynn steers me into the little waiting room. No one is in it at this hour. No one is usually in it.

"I wish Holley Jo could visit me." It comes out without warning and startles me.

"If she can't visit you, maybe you can visit her," Dr. Lynn says. "You'll be out of here soon."

My breath catches as though someone had just popped me in the stomach. I hadn't thought about being able to see Holley Jo again. The idea is so welcome, so exciting, so unexpected that I cling to it, wanting to shout with it; and I think, *This is what it feels like to be happy*. I had honestly forgotten.

Dr. Lynn sits on one of the hard plastic chairs, and I plop on the brown vinyl sofa, which lost its springs generations ago.

"Maybe I could drive you there on my day off," she says. "I'd love to see some of the hill country. This part of Texas is new to me."

She adjusts the green skirt that pokes out from under her white coat.

"Thank you," I say. "Oh, thank you!" And tightly wound in this crazy ecstasy of joy, I say something as insanely foolish as I feel. "In that green skirt, with your white coat, you match old grasshopper legs."

Her eyes widen. "Who in the world is old grasshopper legs?"

"Dr. Paull. He's got the weirdest green plaid slacks."

"Oh," she says. She blinks rapidly a few times and stares at a spot over my head.

"It's just a private joke. If you saw those green slacks, you'd agree with me."

"Not necessarily." There's a lot of pink under those freckles.

I suddenly catch on. "Dr. Lynn, is there something between you and Dr. Paull?"

It's funny to see someone who is usually so self-controlled look embarrassed. "I don't think we want to discuss my private life."

"He's not good enough for you."

Her chin lifts. "What do you mean by that?"

"He's kind of a pill. That's what I mean."

"He's a dedicated doctor. He's serious about his work."

"If he loved you, he'd be happy. Then he'd act nicer to his patients."

"No one's talking about love," she says. She leans forward. She's in command again. "Dina, you can be a big help with Julie. It's obvious that she knows something she doesn't want to tell us. In fact, we know very little about her."

"She doesn't talk to me, either."

"What about this man who is frightening her?"

"When she woke during the night, she was scared to death. She said he was in the room."

"Jack told me about the nightmare."

"Jack?"

"Oh. Dr. Paull."

"That's one thing I don't like about him. He just assumed it was a nightmare. He didn't listen. I told him it felt as though someone was in the room. I was scared, too. But he didn't listen to me. He didn't listen to either of us."

She thinks a moment. Finally she says, "There is a possibility someone could have been in the room. The nurses can't see everything that's going on at every minute."

"Thanks for having an open mind. Julie was afraid that the man in the supply room was this guy, too."

"What does she call him?"

"Sikes. She insists that he killed her father."

"She says she cried when her father died. Have you seen her cry?"

"Yes, and I was glad when she did. It sort of frightened me when she knew her parents were dead but she didn't cry."

"Sometimes it's hard for people to cry. Sometimes they're in a temporary state of disbelief."

"Can a state like that come and go?"

"I don't understand, Dina. What are you asking?"

"Well, sometimes Julie lets down, and then she's like one of the kids at the home. But at other times I get the impression that her head is so filled with terrible thoughts that the fear has pushed her into a corner of her own mind, and she's afraid to come out."

"Okay," she says. "I know what you mean."

"She's so afraid of this Sikes that she can't feel what she's supposed to feel about losing her parents."

"I told you that you'd be a help," she says. "This gives me something to work with."

"She said she should have been killed, too. Apparently Sikes tried to kill all of them. If someone did this and he's after Julie, shouldn't somebody care? Shouldn't somebody try to stop him?"

"Yes," she says. "A detective asked to question Julie, and I requested that he wait until after I had talked with her. He'll probably come by soon after I phone him. I'll tell him exactly what you told me. He'll know what to do."

She gives me that wide smile. "Want to talk about yourself? How you feel about leaving the hospital?"

"Dr. Lynn, I can't go yet." And I tell her about this dumb promise I made to Julie.

"Why do you think it was a 'dumb' promise?"

"Because I don't want to get mixed up in anyone else's life."

"Yet you are, and by your own choice. You could have rejected her on the spot."

"Don't try to look inside me."

"I want you to look inside yourself."

I get up from that sagging sofa and walk to the other side of the small room, keeping my back to her. "When I look inside myself, I see a monster. It's an eyeless thing with a gaping mouth and a thousand claws, and it's churning inside me and eating away at me."

She is suddenly beside me. "Your disease is in remission. You know that. You must accept that."

"I'm trying to accept it. But I know the thing is there, and even if it's in a cage for now, someday it will be strong enough to break the cage and get out."

"Dr. Cruz was honest with you. He expects you to be honest with him. Your being honest means believing that you will be one of the survivors. There's a fine chance of survival now. In the years to come everyone who gets Hodgkin's disease may be cured."

"I hate my body for doing this to me!"

She puts an arm around my shoulders, not like a doctor, like a friend. Finally she says, "I'll do what I can to help find a place where you and Julie can be together."

"At least for a while," I say. "Until she has other people she can trust."

"Agreed."

"Thanks." Now I can smile at her. "Let's go back, so you can call that detective. I want someone to start working on this problem. If Sikes is frightening Julie, then the police should find him."

It's after dinner when the detective arrives.

I'm not surprised to see Dr. Lynn with him. But Julie is afraid of the man. She's a little, shrunken, shivering person in that bed, eyes stretched wide in a tight face.

"I'm here to help you, Julie," he tells her. "I'm Roger MacGarvey."

He looks like his name. He's a broad, muscular man with dark, thick hair. He reminds me of those big men with kilts and bagpipes in the eighth-grade geography book. Even at that age Holley Jo and I could appreciate those great, burly legs. I wonder how Roger MacGarvey would look in kilts. It's an interesting thought.

"Julie, tell me the names of some of your relatives. You've got a grandmother? An aunt?"

His pen poises over his notebook, but she shakes her head.

"You must have someone."

"No," she says.

"Maybe it's someone you haven't met. Did your mother or father ever talk about a cousin, or a brother? Someone in another city?"

Negative.

"Julie," he says, "we need to find someone who can take care of you."

Her eyes flicker to me, where I am perched on the edge of my bed, my bare toes playing with the hem of my robe. "I haven't got any relatives," she says.

MacGarvey stares at his notepad for a few moments. Then he raises his head. "Julie, you must have gone to school. Could you tell us the name of the last school you went to?"

"I went to lots of schools," she answers. It surprises me that now she's willing to talk. "We moved a lot. Sometimes we lived in apartments. Sometimes we lived in a mobile home. I didn't like the mobile home."

"Tell me the name of your school."

"There were so many schools. I don't remember. There was Brookhollow. I remember Brookhollow. I was in the second grade, and we stayed long enough so that I could go to the Halloween carnival. My teacher was nice, but she left to have a baby, and I cried because she was the only one who told me I was smart and put gold stars on my papers."

"What city was Brookhollow in?"

Her forehead crinkles. Then those clear blue eyes focus on his, and she says, "It might have been in Tennessee, or Georgia. I was only in the second grade."

"What grade are you in now?"

"Fourth. No, third. I'll be in fourth grade next fall. But I haven't been to school for a long time. My mother just gave me lots of books to read. I'm a good reader."

MacGarvey pauses, and Dr. Lynn steps forward. "What kind of books do you like to read, Julie?"

"I like to read about horses," she says, "and ghosts." There is something about that high-pitched, thin voice in this quiet room that makes me uncomfortable.

"Your doctor told me that you just moved to

San Antonio," MacGarvey says. "Can you give me your address?"

"It was just for a week. About a week, I think. We lived in an apartment house near the freeway."

"We have a number of freeways in San Antonio, Julie. Can you describe the apartment house for me?"

She thinks for a minute. "It's white. It looks like most apartment houses look. It's ugly, and it has ugly furniture. Most apartment houses have ugly furniture."

"Is it near a shopping center?"

"Yes."

"What kind of stores do you remember in the shopping center?"

She names two chain stores that must be in every shopping center in the United States.

"What can you tell us about your father, Julie? What kind of jobs did he have?"

"He was an auto mechanic," she says.

"Do you know where?"

She shakes her head again.

"Did your mother ever tell you what kind of work she did while your father was in jail?"

The blue eyes spark, and she struggles up from the pillow. "My father was never in jail!"

MacGarvey looks at Dr. Lynn, then back at Julie. "Please try to think of something that will help us, Julie. We need to know where your parents come from. We want to find someone who will take good care of you."

"I can't think of anything."

"For now can you give me the names of some cities and towns where you recently lived? Any addresses?"

She hesitates, and he adds, "You're nine years old. You're old enough to know where you've lived during the last year."

"We were in a trailer park in Miami, Florida, in January and February," she says. "I think it was named Seabird. And then we were in another trailer park in a little town in Louisiana for two weeks, but I can't remember its name. And we stayed in Texarkana in an apartment house, and that's where they sold the mobile home, because my mother was afraid of tornadoes, and she said they hit mobile homes. The apartment house was on a street called—"

She suddenly stops. "We were just there for a week. I don't remember the name of the street, but I think it started with a C. And we lived in some places in Arkansas and Texas."

MacGarvey leans back, resting his pad and pencil on his lap. "Dr. Manning tells me that you think a man named Sikes is responsible for your parents' death, and that you may be in danger from him. Is that right?"

Julie gets white, and I jump to my feet, expecting her to pass out. But she doesn't. Her voice is a hoarse croak as she says, "I was supposed to die in that crash, too. I hate Sikes! I hate him! He killed my father!"

"Where is this man Sikes?" MacGarvey asks. "Where can I find him?"

Julie's voice is so soft now that for a moment I must have misunderstood her, but as she repeats what she just said, I get so scared I grab the bedside table and hold on.

"He's watching us," Julie says. "And he's waiting, because he knows where I am."

CHAPTER

Her eyes move toward the doorway, and the three of us look, too, as though we expected the door to open and someone to walk through.

"He might even be hiding in the hospital," Julie says. "He's good at hiding. The police can never find him."

Dr. Lynn steps up to MacGarvey and nods at him. "I think we can let Julie rest now," she says. "Maybe you'd like to talk to her tomorrow."

"Sure," he says. "Tomorrow." He looks as though he's glad to be leaving, but he takes a moment to study Julie. "Try to think of an address, Julie," he tells her. "Come up with something that will help us."

The two of them leave, and Mrs. Cardenas pops in. She's got two paper cups of ice cream, and she gives them to us. "I was working in the hallway," she says. "I heard some of it."

"I think you know everything that goes on in this hospital," I tell her. The ice cream is cold, and I lick the spoon slowly, letting it numb my lips.

"Probably," she says matter-of-factly. She sits on the end of my bed, and the mattress sags. She grins at Julie. "*Niñita*, how's it going?"

"Okay," Julie says. "I like the ice cream. I liked the fruit juice you brought me, too."

Mrs. Cardenas winks at me. "You missed the fruit juice, Dina, because you were busy walking down the hall with Dr. Lynn. You want fruit juice, you gotta stick around."

I take another mouthful of ice cream, and she says, "Sometimes it happens. A man can hide from the police for a lifetime. I know some people who came over the border when they were young, got jobs, raised families, and now they're old, and the law still hasn't caught up with them."

She pauses for a deep breath. "And a man commits a crime. He can keep moving, too. My brother-in-law, Arturo, tells me that there's lots of crimes that never get solved. It's not like all the detective shows on TV."

Julie is staring into her ice cream cup, rhythmically eating as though there was nothing in the world more important to do.

Mrs. Cardenas goes right to the point. "Julie," she says, "if you know places you lived, all that stuff, you should tell the detective who came here."

"But I don't know," Julie answers.

Mrs. Cardenas nods at me. "*Es una posibilidad.* People on the run don't teach their *niños* addresses and phone numbers. It's safer if the little ones don't know much."

"Is that it? Was your family running away, Julie?" I ask.

"We just kept moving," Julie says. "I hated all the moving."

I hand my empty cup to Mrs. Cardenas. "Will you tell all this to Dr. Lynn? I don't think the doctor, or even the detective, understands."

"They live in a different world," Mrs. Cardenas says. "And they don't ask people in other worlds how it is."

She elaborately shrugs her roundly padded shoulders, but the smile is there, and I suddenly hurt at the thought that she'll leave the hospital, and I'll leave the hospital, and I'll never see her again.

But a stronger, startling thought tramples the first. "Mrs. Cardenas, what are you going to do after you resign from the hospital?"

"Rest my aching back," she says. "The legs don't feel too good, either." She stretches them straight out and studies them, rotating her pudgy ankles. "Carlos—he's my husband—don't bring in much money, but at least it's steady, and we can get along."

"You could make a little extra money," I say, "and have some help besides."

She peers at me sideways, one eyebrow raised.

"How am I gonna do that? Win one of those big contests?"

I lean toward her eagerly. "Take in a couple of foster children—Julie and me."

Julie's mouth is open, and both of Mrs. Cardenas's eyebrows are raised like little banners. The idea has been forming while I've been talking, and I am just beginning to realize what I've said. I'm surprised, too, but it seems to make such good sense. I don't want to spend what time I've got with strangers. I like Mrs. Cardenas. She cares about people. She really likes people. She'd be good for Julie.

I talk fast. "I can drive. I can run errands for you. And I'm a good cook. Julie and I can help you clean house. And I know that you'll get paid for our expenses and something more."

"It's a lot of responsibility," she answers, but I can see her turning the idea around and around, examining it for leaks, as she does the paper juice cartons.

"Ask your husband. See what he thinks."

"Poor old Carlos. When he gets home from his job, he heads straight for the table. And when his stomach is full, he plops himself in front of the TV and snores and snoozes until it's time for bed. What would he do with a couple of noisy kids around the house?" The hearty laughter that bubbles out is so contagious that I have to smile. "I guess you're not exactly a couple of noisy kids, are you?" she adds.

"Do you have room for us in your house?" I ask.

"Oh, sure," she says. "That's no problem."

For the first time Julie speaks up. She crawls to the foot of the bed and sits cross-legged, tucking down her oversize hospital gown, which twists around her. "Do you have a real house?"

"You bet," Mrs. Cardenas says. "It's not the kind to go on the cover of a magazine, but it looks good to me. It's a wooden house and it's painted white, and there's a green trim around the windows and lots of oleander in the front yard."

"What color?"

"Pink," she says. "That nice, bright pink that's like the inside of a watermelon in the middle of July. And my dining room is fancy because I've got my grandmother's hand-carved table, and a red glass bowl full of those silk fruits I made in a crafts class at the center. And my Aunt Lila crocheted doilies for the backs and arms of the red plush chairs in the living room, so it looks good, too."

"What's a doily?" Julie asks.

"It's a little fancy white thing," Mrs. Cardenas says. She thinks for a moment. "Well, you'll just have to see for yourself. I'm not that good at describing things."

"Yes, you are," I tell her. "I can see your rooms, and I like them."

"I didn't tell you about the porch, and that's the best part. Along the front of the house is a porch with a white rosebush climbing up one side. I can sit on my porch and look down to Woodlawn Lake. The joggers run around the lake in the early mornings and when the day cools down near evening time, little boys and girls come to the casting pond and throw in their lines." She smiles, and this smile is for herself. "It's a nice place to live."

"It's a real house," Julie murmurs.

For a few minutes each of us shuts out the others. I try to picture myself in this house, but I keep moving through the living room to the back, searching for a quiet room, a place where I can be alone to sleep.

Mrs. Cardenas gives herself a little shake and hops from the bed. "Well," she says, "I gotta get home, or Carlos will sit down at the table before dinner is ready, and he won't like that at all."

She picks up Julie's ice cream cup. "I'll ask Carlos what he thinks."

"Will you talk to Dr. Cruz, too? He can give you all the information."

"Maybe it would work. Maybe not. I'll think about it." But her eyes, as she smiles at me are not counting the pros and cons. They are the eyes of a friend.

Later, when the darkened room shows only the slim strip of light from under the door, I linger before going to sleep. This is my private part of the day, and I cling to it jealously. Julie's breathing is a steady snuffle, a muffled metronome. Occasional footsteps click in the hallway, and nasal voices hum garbled words down at the nurses' station.

It's now I can tuck my unwanted body between the sheets and leave through the gateways of my mind.

I can smell the soft earth around the pole beans in the yard of my home in the hills. I finger the silky tassels of corn, budding on the young stalks. A lone bee burrows into the moon-dipped pollen of the ligustrum bushes, ignoring me as I silently, invisibly glide to the main house, slipping through the wall, resting my cheek against the smoothly polished wood molding around the front entrance.

Thick, yellow light pours from the open door of Dr. Martin's office, but I'm not tempted to step inside and see his balding head bent over the perpetual stack of papers on his desk. I'm here to keep strong the bonds between me and the home I have always known, and that bond is strongest in my own room.

My bed is so tidy, so sterile. I sit on it, tucking my legs under me, wishing I could rumple the faded chenille spread, dent the pillow with my presence.

Holley Jo rolls her hair on big pink sponge rollers. She doesn't use the mirror propped against her desk. Her history book is open against the mirror, and she mumbles to herself as she reads. Exam time. I had forgotten. End of term, end of school, panic of endless facts poured into our brains. I wish I could help her. We always studied together. Question and answer. It was a good system.

We did so much together. "Two little pea pods," Carlotta used to call us, and we'd giggle because she got her clichés so mixed up.

I smile as I remember the time Holley Jo and I were thirteen and decided to become fashion models. We practiced walking with chins held high, noses uptilted, in a gliding kind of step we thought models would use. "We're perfect," Holley Jo said, so we went into town to the JCPenney store and walked through their fashion department, hoping people would think we were real models. People did stare, especially when Holley Jo, with her head so high she couldn't see where she was going, fell over a stroller, and I landed on top of her.

And I think of the time she got a part in the sophomore play. It wasn't a very big part, and all she had to do was say a few lines and munch one or two potato chips that were set out for hors d'oeuvres. I helped her memorize her lines as Gwendolyn until I was sick of them, but she was terrified she'd forget them on opening night.

"You won't forget," I insisted.

"I will! I know I will!"

"I'll stand in the wings," I said. "If you forget your lines, I'll whisper them to you."

It took a push to get her onstage. I remember that. But she came in on cue. Just one thing was wrong. She forgot to reach for a potato chip.

"Potato chips!" I whispered as loudly as I dared. "Don't forget the potato chips!"

"Potato chips?" she murmured, picking up the bowl and staring at it.

"Won't you sit down, Gwendolyn?" one of the characters said.

Holley Jo did, still holding the bowl of potato chips, which she proceeded to put in her lap, eating the chips like crazy, until the bowl was empty. She didn't forget her lines, but sometimes it was hard to understand what she was saying.

I lean back against the wall and watch her. Holley Jo, I miss you. But I may be coming to see you. Dr. Lynn said she'd take me. I've changed since we were last together. I hope you'll look at me—the real Dina, the inside Dina. I don't want to see the shock of my body in your eyes.

The window is open, and the warm breeze that lifts the curtains carries the fragrance of newly cut grass. There is a cricket underneath the window, punctuating Holley Jo's monotonous murmuring. I'm content now, and I'm sleepy.

I am always surprised when morning comes. There were days when mornings seemed to bring pain and nausea and firm voices saying, "You're doing fine, Dina." Slowly the gentle mornings followed. This is one of them, and I greet it with relief.

The rattling carts; the slapping, hurrying feet; the chattering voices are filling the hall. But there's another sound, a closer sound.

Julie is humming. It's nasal and thin, but I can recognize the tune: "As Long As He Needs Me." I try not to move. I don't want to disturb her. This was the song that her mother sang, and in her own way Julie must be mourning her mother.

But the door slams open, and Mrs. Marsh sails in, popping thermometers in our mouths, taking pulses, and pulling the curtain between our beds so defin-itively I look to see if there's a rule printed on it.

"You can get up and shower by yourself today, Julie," she says. "Remember the red button on the wall of the bathroom if you need me."

"Don't dawdle," Mrs. Marsh tells me. "The break-fast trays will be here in fifteen minutes." She leaves a wake of quivering air currents that take a few moments to settle.

"If you want to use my shampoo, it's on the shelf," I tell Julie.

"You go first," Julie says. "I'm always poky, and I don't much like breakfast anyway."

So I shower and shampoo and towel-dry my hair in record time. Over my pink cotton underpants, standard regulation at the home, I put on a fresh hospital gown. I'd like to wear my own nightgowns, but there's no one who can do my laundry for me.

It's Julie's turn next, and she's right. She is poky. The trays come, and I nibble at the stuff I like best. The bacon, the fruit cup. Why do they serve those bowls of gluey white lukewarm cereal? Who eats it? Hundreds of patients get it on their trays. All of them send it back. Bowls and bowls of gluey white stuff returned to the hospital kitchens.

There is a knock, and Dr. Cruz comes in. He's early. "I like to see you smiling," he says. He stands at the foot of the bed. "How's it going?"

"Pretty good. I'm so glad to be off those chemo-therapy shots. I hate the awful way they made me feel." I watch his face carefully. "When I'm an outpatient and come back to the hospital for whatever you're going to do to me, I won't have to get those shots again, will I?"

"Each time you come in, we'll give you a blood test, check your lymph nodes, and do a progress report," he answers. "While you're in remission, you won't need those shots. If necessary, the chemotherapist might give you medication by pill."

I groan. "What good will any of that really do?"

"We want to keep you in a state of remission. Eventually, we want to cure you."

"With promises."

He rubs an invisible spot on his left thumb. "Dina, I made you a promise that's going to be hard to keep. I find that it's difficult to find a foster home for you. Finding people who will take care of both you and Julie is going to be almost impossible. And we can't keep you here. Other patients need the beds."

"What does a person have to do to be a foster parent?"

"It's not difficult. The people who apply have to be checked and approved, of course. And the agency keeps checking on them. But being a foster parent—especially to someone who needs medical care—is a big responsibility, and not many people want to take it on. There's an older couple in Balcones Heights who've helped us out before. I was counting on them, but they turned me down. She's having trouble with arthritis and says she isn't up to taking care of anyone now."

So I tell him about Mrs. Cardenas.

He looks hopeful. "I'll leave a message for Mrs. Cardenas to call me as soon as she comes in."

"I think she'll be good for Julie. Julie needs someone to mother her."

"Julie." He looks over at her empty, rumpled bed. "So many patients come through this hospital. We give them whatever care we can, and it's good care. But we can't follow through on everyone. Who knows what Julie needs? We don't have time to find out."

Dr. Cruz glances at Julie's bed again. "She hasn't touched her breakfast tray. Where is she?"

"Taking a shower," I answer. Then I realize that I haven't heard the sound of the water running for quite a while.

I jump out of bed, not caring that all I've got on is this dumb hospital gown with nothing but ties in the back. I clutch it together with one hand, and with the other I hammer on the bathroom door. "Julie! Come on out and eat your breakfast!"

No one answers. I try to turn the knob, but it resists. "Julie!" I call. "Don't lock the door. Julie! Answer me!"

CHAPTER 5

Dr. Cruz is at my side. "These doors don't lock," he says. He takes the knob and tries to turn it, pushing against the door. "She's holding it shut," he grunts and gives a harder turn to the knob.

I can see he's afraid of forcing the door with so much strength that he'd risk knocking Julie to the tile floor.

"Julie," he says, "let go. I'm coming in the door, and I don't want you to get hurt."

The door suddenly flies open. Julie has backed away, and is standing there naked, clutching her towel in front of her.

"Get her a clean gown from the closet," Dr. Cruz tells me, and quietly he adds, "Julie, what's the matter?"

"I heard what you said." Her voice is shrill. "You

said no one would take us together. I don't want to go someplace by myself."

I bring the gown, edging past Dr. Cruz, who is keeping the bathroom door open by standing against it. I hold it out so Julie can slip her hands into it, and I move around her to tie the tapes in the back.

For a moment I stare. Then I close my eyes, trying to breathe evenly. There are welts on Julie's back and buttocks, diagonal and horizontal slashes that look as though she's been whipped.

"Dr. Cruz!"

"Just a minute, Dina," he says, and he turns to Julie. "Climb back in bed and eat your breakfast. You didn't hear all our conversation, or you'd know we haven't given up."

Julie's mood changes abruptly. She obediently walks past him and toward her bed.

"Dr. Cruz! I have to talk to you!" I whisper.

"Not in the bathroom," he answers. "Get your robe and come out in the hall."

"I'll be right back," I tell Julie, feeling as though I need to reassure her every time I step out of her sight.

She simply nods and dips her spoon in the fruit cup.

I struggle into my robe, fumbling with the tie, and run barefooted into the hall, tugging the door shut behind me.

"Her back!" I whisper, although I'm sure she can't hear me. "It's awful! Someone has beaten Julie!"

He nods. "We know. Her doctor saw that when he first examined her."

"But—" I don't really know what I want to ask.

"There's no point now in trying to find out who did it, if that's what is bothering you," he says. "Her parents are dead. The person responsible isn't going to do it again."

"It's terrible to think about someone doing that to a little girl." I rest against the wall. "Isn't there anything we can do?"

"Yes," he says. "You can be her friend. Let her lean on you for a little while."

I stand up straight and scowl at him. "Don't lay this on me. What's she going to do when she gets dependent on me and suddenly I'm not around to pick up her problems for her?"

"I said for just a little while. Remember, it was your idea in the first place."

"Just to be near her, that's all, nothing more. And what about later?"

He starts rubbing his thumb again, and I take a step toward him. "All I want to do right now is go home."

"But you can't." He puts a hand on my shoulder. "You're old enough to accept facts. We think the odds are in your favor, but you're going to have to live a different life-style with regular treatments at the hospital as an outpatient. Those are the facts."

The facts taste bitter. They stick in my throat and swell my tongue and make me want to vomit.

"I'll talk to you later," he says. "And I'll see if

we can't get the rest of your clothes and things sent here from the home."

"I could go there and get them!" I grab his arm. My hands are trembling. "Dr. Lynn said she might —that maybe—" My desire is so deep that I can't speak.

He seems to understand. "Dina," he says, "we'll all do our best."

I go back in the room and stand at the window, gazing over the low hills to the horizon. If I could only steal a cookie from Carlotta, greet the people I've known for so long, laugh once more with Holley Jo. The possibility is so close, so precarious, that I can hardly bear it.

"What are you thinking about, Dina? What's the matter?"

Julie is staring at me with concern. For a few moments I've forgotten her. "I've been thinking of the place where I've grown up. There may be a chance I can go back to visit and get my things."

"You'll stay there."

"No. They won't let me."

"What are they going to do with us?"

When I was nine, I still hoped to be part of a family someday. Dreams have a way of clinging long after they've grown thin and impractical. My world was not a secure one, and I can remember. Nine can be fragile. Ten is a milestone, a strengthening point; but nine needs a helping hand.

I perch on the foot of Julie's bed, facing her. "I don't know where we'll be. I'm hoping that Mrs.

Cardenas and her husband will want to have us. But I know that Dr. Cruz and Dr. Lynn will do their best to find us a home together."

"I'm scared," she says. "Are you?"

"I stopped being scared," I tell her. "One day I just stopped."

"When we live with someone else, will we be like their children?"

"They'll take care of us the way they would their children or anyone's children. And we'll help around the house. Didn't you do dishes and make beds and all that for your parents?"

Surprisingly she shudders. "My mother got mad at me if I didn't do it right."

"No one's going to get mad at you. And I'll be with you. I won't let anyone hurt you." I listen to myself make this promise, and I wonder what I'm doing.

Julie's shoulders relax, and I have to ask, "Who beat you?"

When she doesn't answer, I add, "I know this is what you've been trying to hide from the doctors and the police. But they know."

"I don't want to talk about it. I don't want to talk about Sikes."

"Sikes?" I've spoken too loudly, and I glance around, not wanting anyone to hear. "I don't understand. Where was your father? How could he let this happen?"

Julie's knees are up, and she hugs them tightly. "I told you," she whispers. "Sikes killed my father."

There is a knock, and the door swings wide. It's Detective MacGarvey.

"Good morning," he says.

"Good morning," I answer as I untangle my legs and slide off the bed. "Is Dr. Lynn coming, too?"

"I doubt it." He crooks one finger under the metal tube rim of a chair and easily deposits it next to Julie's bed. "She and a couple of doctors and somebody named Mrs. Cardenas are in an office at the end of the hall. And they're having a very loud conversation, one at a time, with someone on the other end of the telephone."

"Julie!" I say. "They may be talking about our going to live with Mrs. Cardenas!"

"Oh!" is all that Julie answers. She has backed away from MacGarvey as far as she can go, pressing the headboard of the bed with her spine.

MacGarvey lowers himself into the small chair, which wobbles into place. He opens his notebook. "Julie, do you know if your parents were running from someone?" I wonder if he's been talking to Mrs. Cardenas.

Julie just stares at him without answering.

He waits a moment, then tries again. "Tell me about this man you call Sikes," he says. "Was your father afraid of him?"

I break in. "Julie, please answer Detective Mac-Garvey's questions. He wants to help you."

She hesitates for a moment, then says, "I don't think my father was afraid of Sikes. But I know he hated Sikes. Lots of times when I was little, Sikes came to the house."

"How little?"

"I don't know."

"Were you too young to go to school?"

"It's hard to remember."

"What did Sikes do?"

"I don't know. I didn't see him do anything. But my father hated him."

"How do you know this?"

"Because he told my mother he never wanted that man to come to the house again."

There really was a Sikes. There is a Sikes. And it sounds as though Julie's mother— But if it's true that Sikes killed her parents, why? And why did he chase them? And why should he want to kill Julie?

"What did your mother say when your father told her that?" MacGarvey asks.

"She cried. They argued."

"What did they say?"

"I don't remember."

Julie has knotted her fingers in a tight ball under her chin. "Sikes killed my father," she says. "I told you that. I told everybody. He killed my father."

"Can you give me a first name for this man Sikes?"

"Bill Sikes," she says.

The name sounds familiar, as though I'd heard it before. I don't know where. I guess there are more

Bills in the world than anyone could count. There were ten Bills and Billys in my class at school.

MacGarvey folds up his notebook and tucks it in his pocket. "Thank you, Julie," he says. "We may talk another time."

It's not until he leaves that Julie begins to relax.

"Let's walk down the hall," I tell her. "I want to know what's going on in the office."

"I haven't got a robe," she says.

"No problem." I find a second hospital gown in the closet. It's even bigger than the first, so it comes to her ankles. But I put it on with the opening in front, so she's wearing them one on top of the other, back to back. It will never make the fashion scene, but it serves the purpose.

She takes my hand as we walk. Her hand is a thin, five-pronged clamp, and I'm surprised again at her strength. Maybe it's just that I've spent the last few months being weak. There's a contrast.

As we get close to the office, I hear Dr. Cruz saying, "Red tape! All this red tape! Why can't people do things the sensible way?"

"Tell her not to mail the application," Dr. Lynn says. "I'll pick it up. That will save time."

"What do they ask at the interview?" Mrs. Cardenas says. "I thought the hard part would be to get Carlos to say yes. But he said if it would keep me home, then he'd go for it. Now we gotta be interviewed. I don't know what they'll ask."

"TB test, food handler health card, fire inspection," Julie's doctor says. "All that will take time."

"I got a sister-in-law who's a social worker for the county," Mrs. Cardenas tells him. "I'll call Dolores and see what she can do."

"It may take a few days," Dr. Lynn says, "but it's going to work out well for everyone. Mrs. Cardenas, we're so glad that—"

I step into the small office, pulling Julie with me. "We're going to stay with you, Mrs. Cardenas? Really? Is it true?"

She laughs. "*Es verdad.*"

"It's just a matter of getting through some forms, interviews, home checks—that sort of thing," Dr. Cruz explains.

"And in the meantime, we can get you both some clothes," Dr. Lynn says.

"What do you think? They worked it out with the office here to give me two weeks vacation time, so I still get paid, but I can quit at the end of the week!" Mrs. Cardenas's cheeks are flushed, and she wiggles as though she wanted to bounce up and down. "I hope I get my party," she adds.

'What party?"

"When somebody who works here leaves, the people on the floor usually have a cake and some punch. A real nice party."

"You'll certainly have your party," Dr. Lynn says.

I should be glad that Mrs. Cardenas wants us. But for some reason I am sad. Why? I try to move back, to look inside my mind, to find this mixed-up person who lives inside, but there are too many people in the room, too much chatter. I am locked into the now, planted firmly in the here.

Dr. Lynn has moved beside me. She takes my other hand and leads me into the hall. Julie comes, too, with her grip that won't let go.

"On Thursday, Jack—Dr. Paull—and I are off duty. Would you like us to take you to the home where you lived, so you can see your friends? Get your things?"

"Oh, yes!" Thursday is real. A square on the calendar. A time I can count on. Three days away. "Yes," I repeat. "I'll be ready."

"Can I come, too?" There is a tugging on my arm.

I'd like to cry out at Julie, "I don't want to be your mother!" but instead I take a long breath and wait.

Dr. Lynn picks up the answer. "I think it would be nice if Julie came with us. After we drop you off to see your friends, Dr. Paull and I can show her some of the countryside."

Thank you thank you thank you thank you. "You'd like that, Julie. You wouldn't know anyone at the home."

Julie thinks a moment, then nods. "Okay."

"I'll let them know we're coming," Dr. Lynn says. "And I'll make sure they give the message to Holley Jo."

The days go slowly. Dr. Lynn comes in each day to talk to Julie, and Mrs. Cardenas pops in as often as the witch on a temperature gauge who announces the rain in the dripping months of autumn. But Mrs. Cardenas's announcements are all positive. Her sister-in-law got the paperwork speeded up, and her cousin, Carmen, is dating someone in the fire department who got the Cardenas house inspection at the head of the list. There's a slight delay on the food handler license because none of the relatives have connections there, but Dr. Cruz has used his deep-voiced authority to try to get things moving in that department.

"After my party on Friday," Mrs. Cardenas tells us, "you'll come home with me."

Wednesday, and Dr. Lynn has brought Julie some clothes. I have my jeans and blouse, which I wore when I came here. I put them on and stare at myself in the mirror. These are clothes that fit another girl who lived in another world. What am I doing, trying to put my skinny bones in pants so large I have to hold them up? In a blouse that droops over the shoulders and flaps around my waist?

Mrs. Cardenas shakes her head when she sees me. "This is the place for a needle and thread," she says. Somehow the juice cartons get delivered to patients in record time, and she comes back to our room with everything she needs to pin and tuck and sew and cut. I try the clothes on again, and this time they fit.

Thursday moves from a long, sleepless night into a sudden rush of morning. The air is still, the sky is golden. I can't eat. I am dressed and waiting in the chair by the window before Julie has even finished her breakfast.

"Hurry up," I tell her.

"You keep saying that," she complains. "Dr. Lynn won't be here for a long time."

She dawdles, so I help her. I pull her twiglike arms through the sleeves of her T-shirt and jam the neck of it down over her head.

"Ouch!" she says. "You messed up my hair."

"I'll brush it for you." More slowly, more gently, I brush her pale hair, reminding myself that she's only nine years old.

Dr. Lynn and Dr. Paull arrive together. His professional dignity is punctured with the smiles he keeps giving Dr. Lynn. He looks much nicer when he smiles.

"We have a great day for a drive," he says.

And we do. The wild flowers are gone now, but the air is fragrant with sun-warmed field grass and the prickly-sour smell of new oak leaves.

"I'd like us to be friends, Dina," Dr. Paull says.

"Okay," I answer.

It's hard for him to unbend, but I can see that he's trying, for Dr. Lynn's sake. Then he tells us some fourth-grade jokes that he probably memorized from a book for kids. He's just not with it. He's wearing those green plaid slacks again, and it's awfully hard not to think of him as "old grasshopper legs."

The highway passes the farms on the outskirts of Boerne and climbs past the exit to Kerrville. We chat about a number of things. What, I don't know. My mind is already at the home.

Holley Jo will be waiting for me. She'll be wearing shorts, her legs already tanned, and she'll brighten like the floodlights on the baseball field when she sees me coming. She'll run to meet me, and we'll hug each other and laugh, and she'll try to tell me everything that has happened since we last were together. It will be like always. And I need it. I need it to happen just this way. I need her to say, "Oh, Dina! Welcome back! I've missed you so much!"

It takes another hour before we are close enough so that I can recognize things: the old white house where the farm-market road cuts across the highway, the windmill that has been rotting away forever, the road to the right that leads to the home.

I perch on the edge of my seat. It's hard to breathe. Dr. Lynn smiles and says something to me, but I don't hear her. I don't want to hear. In a moment we'll round the curve, and I'll see Holley Jo.

The car makes a wide swing, and I grip the seat in front of me. There is the main building. There is the porch. I am able to breathe again. I give a shout. There is Holley Jo, pacing in front, watching the road.

She stops and stares. As we get closer, she waves.

She runs toward the car. And I am out and running toward her before the car has come to a complete stop.

My arms are wide. "Holley Jo!" I shout. "I'm back!"

She falters, and there is such shock on her face that I stop, too. For an instant we stare at each other, unable to cross an invisible barrier that has sprung up between us.

At first I don't understand. "Holley Jo?"

She looks the way she did last summer when she managed to take a young bird away from one of the yard cats, and she held it in her hands and knew it was too late.

When she speaks, her voice is a whisper. "Oh, Dina," she says. "Is it you?"

CHAPTER

6

Dr. Lynn is out of the car now. She has one arm around my shoulders, and she propels me toward Holley Jo. "I'm Dr. Lynn Manning," she says. "I'm so happy to meet you, Holley Jo, because you're Dina's closest friend. She's told me so many lovely things about you."

Holley Jo has wiped the shock from her eyes. She reaches out and hugs me, but gently, as though she's afraid I'm going to crack into little pieces.

"You don't know how much I've missed you," she tells me.

I answer, "And I've missed you."

"Everyone's waiting to see you, but I said I wanted to be the first."

"I'm glad." I kick at a little brown bug that is trying to crawl on my sandal.

"Carlotta baked a huge cake for you."

"She sent me a card."

"Mrs. Pettigrew said to say hello for her. She left this week to live with her daughter."

"There's so much I want you to tell me. Everything that's gone on since I left."

Up until now our words have politely skirted each other, keeping a distance, moving in self-conscious little circles. But Holley Jo suddenly grins. "Guess what! Daisy's getting married! To one of the Parker brothers. The gooney one."

We laugh, and time is back in place.

Dr. Lynn says, "We'll pick you up about two o'clock, Dina."

I wave as they leave. A small white face stares at me from the backseat. I refuse to think about Julie right now. This is where I've wanted to be for so long, and I'm not going to think of anything or anyone else.

As we enter the main building, Dr. Martin and his wife come to meet me. Her broad, toothy grin hasn't changed. Nothing has changed, except me.

Everyone swarms into the room, and I'm pulled into the dining room. Someone has fastened balloons and a banner saying "Hi, Dina" around the door to the dining room. There's pink punch, and a cake, and laughter, and all of them looking at me through glittery glass eyes that hide their feelings. It's a nice party. I didn't expect a party. And I'm tired. So tired.

People are drifting into little groups, and talking

about baseball games and how glad they are the semester has ended, and who has to go to summer school. I tug at Holley Jo's arm and whisper, "Could we go to our room for a little while?"

"Sure," she says. "I know you're tired." So I must show how I feel, and I hate my body even more for not being strong enough to hide its horrible secret.

My feet have become so heavy. One step at a time. That's the way. Try to keep pace with Holley Jo, who is awkwardly trying to keep pace with me. My whole body is exhausted, so unwilling to move. Here are the stairs. I can make it. I will I will I will. There is a room up there. A room with my bed in it. And I can rest. My mind pulls and pushes and prods this body, and it obeys.

"I'll get the door," Holley Jo says.

My bed is nearest the door, and I flop on it gratefully, closing my eyes, feeling the pieces of my body settle into place again.

"I'm sorry," I murmur. "Sometimes I get so tired."

"Just lie there as long as you want," she says. "Ellen won't mind."

"Ellen?" My eyelids flip open.

I'm on a yellow-and-green-printed bedspread. I roll on my side and stare at the room. It's yellow, and there are curtains with a ruffle in this same yellow, trimmed in green.

"Everything's changed!" I cry.

"The Women's Gospel Committee decided to

redecorate this wing," Holley Jo says. "I don't much like it. I wish they'd picked blue."

"Ellen?" I ask. "Did they give my bed to Ellen Greeley?"

Holley Jo squirms and twists her feet around the chair at her desk. "They did some shifting. They said you wouldn't be back."

"I guess they had to. It's just that in my mind this has always been my bed and our room."

She leans forward eagerly. "If—when—you get better and come back, I know they'll put you in here, if you want."

I lie on my back and stare at the ceiling.

"Tell me about Rob."

"He's a nothing."

"Who's he dating?"

She shrugs and gives me a quick look. "Debbie, I guess."

"It's okay," I tell her. "I'm over him."

"Did he ever write you?"

"Rob held an early funeral for me. It was easier for him that way."

"Dina!" she says. "Don't talk like that!"

"Then tell me about Daisy and her wedding. Isn't the one she's marrying named Floyd?

"Yes," she says with a rush of words, "and they're going to be married in the Clarewood Baptist Church next month, and Daisy wants daisies in her bridal bouquet, and I think Pamela is going to be her only attendant because Floyd's mother is picking up the bills, and—"

The wedding is in this room, and the bride wears a dress that matches the bedspread and curtains. "Ugly!" I whisper, and everyone stares. The wedding cake is pink, and around the top is written *Hi, Dina. Good-bye, Dina.* I don't like this wedding, and I wish I hadn't come. All the hollow places inside of me are filled with sadness.

Through a faraway humming I hear Holley Jo saying, "She's been asleep."

"But you've both missed lunch."

"I didn't want to wake her up. She looks so—so—I just had to let her sleep."

"You've been sitting here with her all this time?"

"Of course! I want to be with her!"

I open my eyes. Mrs. Martin is standing at the foot of my bed, watching me. "Your friends have come to pick you up," she says.

I struggle to a sitting position and cry out, "Oh, no! I didn't want to sleep!"

"It's okay," Holley Jo says. She comes to sit beside me.

"There was so much I wanted to talk about."

"Next time, when you're feeling better."

Mrs. Martin's face stretches into that toothy smile. "I'll serve your friends some iced tea, and I'm sure there's some of the cake left. That will give you and Holley Jo a chance to chat while you pack your things."

She closes the door as she leaves. I look around the unfamiliar yellow room again. "I had wanted everything to be the same."

Holley Jo tries to look cheerful, but I can see the traces of red around her eyes. "Nothing stays the same. Each year is different. Next year we'll be seniors and graduate and—"

"I'm a semester behind you now," I say.

"Oh. Well, you know, that we'll probably be going to different colleges—wherever we can get scholarships—and we'll be moving away from the home, and things won't be the same. You know that."

She jumps up and drags a cardboard box from the closet. "I folded up your clothes and put them in here. And there are the things from your desk in a smaller box inside. I was very careful with them. I packed them so neatly you'll be proud of me."

"I wish I had something of value to give you," I tell her. "Something of mine that would last forever, so you'll never forget me."

"How could I forget you? We've been sisters. We'll always write to each other and have vacations together. Remember all our plans? We're going to take a cruise through the Caribbean, and fly to London and visit all the castles that have ghosts in them, and go someplace where they have lots of snow and learn to ski." She stops, and her voice quavers. "You have to get better, Dina."

"We'd better go down," I finally say.

"I'll carry the box."

"Maybe Dr. Lynn will bring me back for another visit." I try a smile. "Next time I won't fall asleep."

"It doesn't matter. I was glad to be with you, no matter what."

Down the stairs. It's easier now. Some of my energy has come back. I follow Holley Jo into the dining room, where Julie stares at me over a mustache of pink frosting.

Dr. Paull leaps up to take the box from Holley Jo. He looks surprised that it isn't heavier.

"We had hamburgers," Julie says. "In Fredericksburg."

Everyone is introduced, and Dr. Lynn says, "We'll have to leave now, or we'll get to the city in time to be caught in the rush-hour traffic."

"Please come again," Holley Jo says. "Please bring Dina back to us."

"Maybe in a few weeks," Dr. Lynn says. "We'll see how our schedules are set up."

There are all the little good-bye things to say and thanks for the rest of the cake, which Carlotta has wrapped for me to take and nearly squashes in her pillowed hug.

Holley Jo's good-bye is the last word I hear as the car swings around the driveway and pulls onto the road. Anger swells through me like the blue norther winds that strip the sky as they rush through winter. It's not fair. Even my retreat has been taken from me. I think of my room, and all I can see now are the yellow walls, the stiff gauze curtains, the tidy green and yellow spreads, which have obliterated any part of me that clung to that room.

"Well, well," Dr. Paull says into the silence. "Dina, you must tell us what you did today. Did you have a good time?"

I am trying to dredge up words through a deep pain, but Dr. Lynn quickly says, "I think we should let Julie tell Dina what we did."

Julie turns toward me. Whoever wiped off her face forgot a spot of frosting over the left corner of her mouth. It wiggles as she talks. "We went to a park," she says. "There were swings and slides, but the slides were too hot. And when we got hungry, we bought hamburgers. Mine had pickles and onions on it. And we did a lot of riding around in the car, and I got tired of all that riding."

Dr. Lynn laughs. "We saw quite a bit of the hill country, and I like it." She rattles on about Texas and what she's learned about Texas history. Grateful to her, I lean back against the seat and close my eyes. Good-bye, Holley Jo. Good-bye, yellow room.

"The day after tomorrow we go to Mrs. Cardenas's house," Julie tells me. She slips her hand into my left hand. "It's a real house," she adds. "I've never lived in a real house. Have you?"

"No," I answer.

The car gives a sudden swerve and speeds up. "There's that fool driver again!" Dr. Paull snaps.

"I recognize the car. I thought we'd seen the last of him near Fredericksburg."

"Surely he wouldn't be following us," Dr. Lynn says.

Julie's eyes grow too large for her face, and I know what she's thinking.

I twist around and see a dark green sedan behind us. He's tailgating, and he's all over the road.

"Maybe you should slow down and let him get past," Dr. Lynn says.

Dr. Paull is hunched forward, concentrating on the wheel. "This is a lonely stretch out here," he says. "I'm not about to give him the chance to force us over."

"You think he wants to rob us?"

"I don't know what he has in mind."

It's like watching a movie, but we're suddenly the actors. I've seen this before, over and over on television. Two cars, careening down the road, the one behind surging forward, just missing any cars coming up the other side, falling back and trying again.

Our car lurches so violently that Julie and I are thrown across the seat. The car wobbles, slows, and Dr. Paull mutters something under his breath.

Julie starts to cry. "That was Sikes!"

"Did you see him?" I manage to pull myself up and watch the green car speeding out of sight around the next curve.

"I know it was Sikes!"

Dr. Lynn turns around. "How do you know, Julie?"

"Because I know."

"That idiot tried to force us off the road," Dr. Paull says.

"Did anyone get the license number?"

"No."

"Did any of us get a good look at him?" Dr. Lynn asks.

No one answers. We drive in silence.

We're close to the junction where the road meets the highway into San Antonio when Dr. Paull shouts, "Look!"

Ahead is the dark green car, tilted drunkenly on the shoulder of the road. A highway patrol car has nosed in ahead of it.

Dr. Paull pulls to the side of the road and turns off the ignition. "I'm going to talk to that officer," he says. "I want to report what happened to us."

Julie flies forward and grabs him around the neck so tightly that he coughs and gurgles before he can break her hold.

"Don't go out there!" she says. "Sikes will hurt you!"

He sidles out the door, keeping a firm grip on her hands. "If it is Sikes," he says, "then we'll see that the officer keeps him in custody."

"But—"

"I'm not afraid of Sikes."

I put an arm around Julie. The three of us watch Dr. Paull approach the patrolman. We can see them talking. Now the driver of the green car is spread-eagled against the side of his car. His head is down.

In a few moments Dr. Paull walks back to us.

"He's just a kid," Dr. Paull says, as he drops into the driver's seat. "He's high on something. Isn't sure where he is or what he's doing. They think it's a stolen car."

We are back on the road again and entering the highway before he adds, "Julie, do you want to tell us more about this man Sikes?"

"No," Julie says. "I don't want to talk about him."

"It would help if you could describe him, tell us why you're so afraid of him."

"No!"

She is wedged against me, and I feel the current that stiffens her body. Her fingers in mine are hot. "Calm down," I tell her. "Don't be scared. It wasn't Sikes."

Dr. Lynn and Dr. Paull begin to talk in low voices, so I tune them out. I keep patting Julie's hand until I feel her relax.

"It wasn't Sikes." She repeats my words to herself.

Who is Sikes? Why does he come wrapped in terror? What does he want from Julie?

I look down at the child beside me and ask myself one more unanswerable question: How much does Julie want from me?

CHAPTER

7

The day has been too much for me, and as we return to the hospital, I try to become vivacious. Sparkle, bubble, put on a false face. Please, may I go again? See, it was good for me. Please, look only into my eyes, where I'm forcing all my energy, and don't notice the blue shadows under the transparent skin.

Dr. Lynn's arm is around me. She is damp and warm and smells of stale cologne. "Take it easy, Dina. Get some rest now."

"I'm not a bit tired."

But she knows. "Our emotions can sometimes make us more tired than our physical problems. You had a pretty fair amount of stress today. The first time back to see your friends can be difficult in some ways. Next time will be easier for you."

"Will there really be a next time? You'll take me again?"

"Yes," she answers. "When you're ready."

"And when we have time." Grasshopper legs has put on his starched white manner without benefit of starched white coat. Here in his environment he is once again the serious medical man. "I'll send the box up to your room," he adds.

"Thank you for taking us," I say, and Julie adds, "Thanks for the hamburgers."

"It was an enjoyable afternoon," he says, but he's looking at Dr. Lynn.

This isn't the kid love I've seen and felt, the Rob-love without roots, not even the can't-wait-to-get-married love like that between Daisy and gooney Parker. I can recognize something else here, and I suppose Dr. Lynn will end up giving Dr. Paull a good part of her life, maybe the rest of it. Is this what her life's all about? I ride up to our floor with Julie clutched in one hand, the package of leftover cake in the other.

"I didn't want to go with them," Julie says. "I wanted to stay with you." Her lower lip curls out in a pout, and she half turns from me.

"You don't own me," I say, but I look at that thin back with the protruding shoulder blades and remember the scars. So I squeeze her hand and say, "I didn't mean to be cross, Julie. I'm tired, and you are, too."

The doors open. As soon as we step into the hall-way Mrs. Cardenas beams and comes toward us.

"Everything's okay with the agency," she says. "Tomorrow's my party, and after that you move in with me!"

"You're a very good person to do this," I tell her. I should feel glad to leave the hospital. Maybe I should feel relieved. But I am too drained to feel anything. I just want to be by myself.

I pull my stiff fingers from Julie's grasp, hand Mrs. Cardenas the cake, and flop on my bed, without even taking off my shoes. Julie goes into the bathroom.

Mrs. Cardenas quickly whispers to me, "Arturo found out the name."

"What name?"

"The name of the woman that William Kaines had raped. It wasn't Sikes. It was one of those long Russian names. I wrote it down, and I still can't say it even when I look at it."

"My guess was wrong," I murmur.

"Don't close your eyes," she says. "You'll go to sleep, and the dinner trays will be along soon."

"I'm not hungry."

I hear the rustle of paper, and Mrs. Cardenas says, "My, what a beautiful cake."

"Help yourself," I tell her. "I don't want any more." Curling, dreaming, withdrawing, head first, I slide into a silent shell.

When I wake, it's into a fire world with a red sunset flooding the room. Julie sits on the end of her bed, a fragile silhouette against the glow. As I lift my head, she hops from the bed and walks into the hallway.

In a moment she is back.

"Where did you go?" I ask her.

"Mrs. Cardenas wanted to know when you woke up. I've been watching you, so I could tell her."

I feel uncomfortable thinking of those serious eyes on me while I was asleep. I get up and stretch, and my stomach growls. I'm surprised to find that I'm hungry.

As though on cue Mrs. Cardenas comes in with a tray. "You need your dinner," she says. "I made them keep this warm for you. Cake is not enough. Your dinner has vitamins in it."

"You're wonderful!" I look at the covered dinner tray and laugh.

She stands back from the tray table, hands on hips. "Well! That's the first time!"

"First time for what?"

"You laughed. That's the first time I heard you laugh since you came to the hospital."

I tuck back inside myself. I don't want people to study me and probe me and count the times that I laugh.

The sun has sucked the color from the hills, leaving them gray and dim. I reach over and pull the string that turns on the light over my bed.

"I've got to go, or my poor Carlos will think he'll never be fed again," Mrs. Cardenas says, and she hurries from the room, stopping in the doorway to add, "That's going to be a good party tomorrow. Everybody on the floor will be there."

Julie sits on the end of my bed. "We're going to the party, too."

I nod, my mouth full of meat loaf.

"The man who brought your box up here wanted to open it for you. He said he could hang up your clothes. But I wouldn't let him. I did it for you."

"You didn't have to do that, Julie. I'll just have to pack them up again tomorrow."

She droops, and that lower lip curls out again. "You want to wear a dress to Mrs. Cardenas's party. You don't want it to be wrinkled."

"Oh. Well, thanks, Julie."

"Your friend didn't pack them very well. I know how to pack better than that." She pauses a moment. "There was another box inside the big box. I put it on the table."

I finish my salad, but just a few bites of the meat loaf is all I can manage. The fat woman who was my roommate for a while used to hobble over to my bed after every meal and eat my custard and pudding and roll and anything I didn't want, until one of the nurses caught her.

"But we don't get enough to eat!" she wailed. "And she doesn't want it!"

Julie says, "What do you keep in that box?"

I swing the table out of the way, lean over, and put the box on my lap.

The box is an old gift box from one of the department stores in San Antonio. What came in it I can't remember—probably a new dress or blouse that I got from the church committee for Christmas. I must have had this box since I was about Julie's age.

As I lift the lid, Julie asks, "What are all those papers?"

"Poetry," I answer. "Written by someone named Rob." I read the poem on the top of the pile. It's not very good. Why had I ever thought Rob was a talented poet?

"I can forgive you for writing a poem that doesn't scan, but for the shallow thought—never!" I say.

"What are you talking about?"

"About what terrible poetry these are. Here. You can reach the wastepaper basket better than I can."

She obediently drops them in and leans over to peer into the box. A small hand flashes in and out and holds up a circle of green. "You have a beautiful ring!"

"It's supposed to be jade, but it only cost a dollar, so I have my doubts about its quality. One year some of us were taken to the San Antonio Spring Fiesta, and we went to La Villita, off the Paseo del Rio, which has all sorts of shops and is part of the old city of San Antonio." I watch her hold it up to the light. "We each bought these rings, but it's been a long time since I've worn mine."

"Why don't you wear it now?"

"It's much too big, and I really don't want to bother with jewelry."

She is examining the ring with such open longing that I follow through and say, "Would you like to have it?"

"Oh, yes!"

"It's going to be too big for you, too."

"Then I'll put it on a gold chain."

"All you need is the chain."

"I've got one."

"Where?" I ask, but she climbs off my bed and onto her own, still examining the ring.

"Can we watch TV?" she asks.

I push the remote-control button for the television, feeling sure that Julie has not suddenly lost interest in the rest of the contents of my box. I have a distinct impression that she's been through it while I slept. It doesn't matter. There's nothing in it of value. I just wish she had been honest with me.

Detective MacGarvey comes by. "I'm on my way home," he says, "and I wanted to make one last try at some information from Julie."

"One last try?" I ask.

"The department can't spare too many man-hours on something like this. Our mechanics couldn't find any sign that the car had been tampered with. It's listed as a one-car accident, and there's no evidence to show otherwise. Whatever possessions they had with them, except for the wallet and driver's license we found on the ground, were destroyed when the car burned."

He sits on the edge of Julie's bed. "Have you thought of anything else to tell me?"

I don't understand why she's afraid of him. She's like a rabbit, trembling and trapped by a fox.

"What have you got there?" MacGarvey asks. He reaches forward and takes the jade ring from her fingers.

"Dina gave it to me."

"It looks a little big," he says. "Here, I can make it fit you." From his pocket he pulls some string and a small pocket knife. He winds the string in a tight, narrow band around one section of the ring. He ties the ends together and cuts them short with his knife. Then he picks up one of the hands that haven't moved and puts the ring snugly on her finger. "How's that, Julie?"

"Thank you," she whispers. She holds her hand high and looks at the ring. For an instant she's visibly pleased.

MacGarvey tucks the rest of the string and the knife back into his pocket. "My wife complains I save everything, but you never can tell when a piece of string might come in handy."

He says to Julie, "We ran a make on William Sikes, and we turned up a few men with that name here and there around the country, but none with a record. Can you tell me where this William Sikes came from?"

"No," Julie says.

"But you can describe him."

"He's big. He has lots of dark brown hair."

"What color are his eyes?"

She thinks a moment. "Maybe they're brown."

"A lot of people could fit that description, Julie. Can you think of any identifying marks?"

"What are identifying marks?"

"Scars, moles, anything that would make him recognizable."

She shakes her head.

"Have you had any other experiences like that first night here, when you thought he might be in your room?"

Julie looks at me. "No," she says.

MacGarvey gets to his feet. "Well, then, I can't think of anything else we can do. If you see him or hear from him, just let us know."

"All right."

He leaves, and Julie's mood changes. "Let's talk about Mrs. Cardenas's party."

"Let's talk about Sikes. Is there a Sikes, Julie? Or did you make him up?"

She stares at me as though she couldn't believe what I've said. I'm surprised that I said it myself. I guess this thought has been pecking the back of my mind, and it's suddenly broken through.

"I told you about Sikes. He killed my father."

"You couldn't even tell the detective what Sikes looks like."

She is on her feet, and she's actually shaking.

"There isn't anything to say about Sikes! I don't want to think about him! I'm afraid of him!"

"Hush," I say, moving quickly, trying to soothe her. "They'll hear you all the way down the hall."

"Sikes is mean! He's terrible!" she says, and now her voice drops so low I can hardly hear her. "I told my mother the things he did to me when she wasn't there, and she said I was lying. And Sikes found out I told her, and he whipped me until my back was bleeding."

"Oh, Julie!" I hug her to me and hold her tightly until she is calm. But I am trembling inside at the horror of what she has told me. And my anger is directed at this man whom I can't even visualize. A name. All I have is a name.

The television is babbling at the other side of the room, and I use it to distract her. "Do you want this program? Or shall we change channels?"

"Let's talk about Mrs. Cardenas's party," she says. She climbs on my bed as though none of our conversation had taken place. "I think they'll have a cake with her name on it," she says. "And you should wear your blue dress because you can tie it in with a belt."

I listen. I make the right responses. But I'm still upset, and I wish I didn't have to go to another party.

It turns out that the party isn't just for Mrs. Cardenas, who fizzes back and forth in the employees' cafeteria like a sparkler on the Fourth of

July. The party is for me, too. And someone has made a small cake for Julie.

Many of the doctors and technicians and even the anesthesiologists are there. Jon, the radiologist who got on a first-name basis with me right from the start, has drawn a funny card for me. Mrs. Marsh has actually brought me a rose from her garden, efficiently pinching off all the thorns.

Nurse's aides, volunteers, and orderlies who have been in and out of my life for the last few months have come to the party. Some of them look different to me, because when I saw them before, it was through a cracked glass of pain. They have come with good wishes, but their real message is good-bye.

These are the people who have done whatever was needed to my body to keep it alive. I should feel grateful, I suppose. I don't. The ending of my life has been stalled, but I know the odds and can figure my chances. Was any of it worth all the trouble?

Finally I leave the party and go back to my room. Too many people coming in and out. Too much noise. Too many. Too much. I want to sleep. No. I want to be as I was before. But fate has zapped me, leaving me with the echo of all those people reverberating in my head.

I wake to find Julie folding my dresses meticulously and putting them in the large cardboard box. It's time to leave. So many good-byes. Mrs. Cardenas's yellow Ford. The ping of cheap gasoline.

Here's the house, but it's dark. Tomorrow, oh, tomorrow, you girls must see the view of the lake from the porch! Doilies. Yes, lots of doilies, and the hum of the air conditioners in the windows. This is my husband, Carlos. Very pleased to meet you, Mr. Cardenas. Thank you for allowing us to stay with you. Thank you for the nice room. *¡No hay de qué!* Twin beds. I wish I could be alone. Take whichever bed you want, Julie. Thank you. *¡Gracias!* Yes, I'm tired. Yes, I'll see you in the morning. My bed has a hollowed-out spot in the middle. This room had been their sons' room before they were grown and moved away. Where away? Far away. Smooth pillowcase against my cheek. I am so tired. So tired.

Murmur from the other bed. "Dina? Dina, are you awake?"

"Umm-hmm."

"Dina, we'll always be together. I'll take care of you. You'll take care of me. And Sikes will never find us."

CHAPTER

3

Morning, and my mind is filled with jumbled questions. What is this room with its blue trumpet flowers dripping from faded wallpaper? Why am I here? Where are the sounds of the hospital carts? It takes me a moment to orient myself, to remember.

Julie's bed is empty, and the small electric clock on the chest of drawers informs me that I've slept through most of the morning. I stretch, enjoying the luxury of awakening when I like, of opening my eyes to trumpet flowers instead of to pale green hospital walls, of smelling hot chocolate from a kitchen and not from a tray.

But guilt crawls in. I had promised to help Mrs. Cardenas. I can't stay in bed another minute. I hurry to get dressed in my jeans and a pink T-shirt that hangs loosely on me. I follow the sound of voices and find Mrs. Cardenas in the kitchen with Julie. Julie is swathed in a gigantic apron over her shorts and shirt, and she is happily drying cups.

"I'm helping Mrs. Cardenas," she tells me. She looks so smug that I have to smile.

"And I'm not," I say. "I didn't mean to sleep so late."

"You need your rest. And now you need some breakfast." Mrs. Cardenas bustles to the gas stove and turns on a circle of blue flame. "We have scrambled eggs, *pan dulce*, and Julie and I made hot chocolate."

I look at the round, sugared loaves of *pan dulce* that are piled on a yellow platter. "I'll get fat."

"You need a little fat. A little fat never hurt anyone."

The guilt clings. "I should have eaten with the rest of you and washed the dishes."

Julie puts the cups she has dried into the cabinet as though she knew where everything went. "Each morning I'll do the breakfast dishes, while you sleep, and you can do the dishes after dinner."

"There are other jobs to take care of," I answer. "What else would you like me to do, Mrs. Cardenas? Dust? Vacuum?"

"Not today," she says. "Today you eat something, then go sit on the porch in the shade. If you feel like it, take a walk down the block to the lake."

So I eat slowly, and it's peaceful in the breakfast

room. There is a honeysuckle vine on the fence next to the window, and a small blur of hummingbird swoops and darts into the blossoms. Mrs. Cardenas answers the phone in her bedroom, and Julie is somewhere in the house. The breakfast room, with its scratched wooden chairs and plastic tablecloth and puddles of sun, belongs to me.

I have no sooner finished, surprised that I've eaten my scrambled eggs, when Julie returns, sweeping my plate to the sink and rinsing it. "I made your bed," Julie says. "And I hung up your clothes in the closet. And I put your other stuff in the top two drawers of the chest, because you're taller than I am."

Why should I feel irritated? She's trying to help. "Thank you," I manage to say. "You didn't need to do all that."

"But I wanted to."

In the distance I can hear the sounds of children playing some kind of game, so I say, "I bet there are some kids your age around here. Mrs. Cardenas would know. When she gets off the phone, why don't you ask her?"

Julie just shrugs. She peels herself out of her apron, stretching on tiptoe to hang it up. "Let's go outside. We can sit on the porch."

She takes my hand and leads me, opening the door and the screen for me. It's really funny in a way. I had thought I was going to have to mother her. Now she's trying to mother me.

There are some chrome and webbing chairs on the porch, but I sit on the steps, my legs in the sun. At the foot of the block, across the boulevard, the strip of lake that is visible is flat blue-gray. A pair of joggers pump their way along the edge, and a boy with a fishing pole strolls past.

Julie sits beside me, and I point out the pole the boy is carrying. Maybe Mrs. Cardenas has something like that left over from when her sons were young. "You could go fishing."

"I don't like to fish."

"You've got a whole summer ahead of you before school starts. We'll have to find some things for you to do, so you can have fun."

"I'll have fun right here. With you."

"But I won't always be with you." What do I say to her?

Her head pivots toward me. "Why not?" she demands. "Are you going back to that place—that home?"

"No." I give a long sigh. "I'll never be able to live there again."

Strangely, her expression changes to one of satisfaction, but she asks, "Then where are you going? Why won't you be with me?"

"Well, Julie, you know I've been very sick." She's only nine. I can't tell her about the percentage who make it, the percentage who don't, and how I'm marking time, waiting until I'm one of the statistics. What do I answer?

But she has taken charge. "Then I'll take care of you," she says. It's as simple as that.

Two guys come down the street. They look to be about my age. One of them is wearing a cutoff net shirt and walks like a football jock. Good body, but I bet he wouldn't know an isosceles triangle from a Bunsen burner. The guy with him is a little shorter, a lot less in the muscle department. He's wearing glasses that look like Rob's glasses. He reminds me of Rob.

They stop, and the jock says, "Hi, skinny."

"Do you always come on so charming?" I shouldn't bother answering him.

The two of them come up the walk to the porch. "Mrs. Cardenas told my mother she was taking in some foster-home kids," he says. "You don't look like a kid."

"I'm a junior in high school."

"You look older than that. You going to our high school next semester?"

I shrug. The other one speaks up. "He's Claudio, and I'm Dave. We live next door to each other— just up the street."

"This is Julie, and my name is Dina."

Dave nods at Julie, but Claudio ignores her. "My sister cut her hair like yours, Dina, and I think it looks awful. Why don't you let yours grow long? You'd be prettier. You're not bad-looking even if you are skinny."

I'd like to date again. But I don't want to go

through another Rob thing. I'll tell them now and get it over with. "I lost all my hair," I say, "when I had chemotherapy treatments. For a while I was bald. Now it's growing out."

Claudio takes a step back, nearly tripping over Dave. "You had chemotherapy? But that's for—"

"Yes." I look directly up at him. "I have Hodgkin's disease. It's a form of cancer."

He moves around Dave, putting more distance between us. "Is it contagious?"

"No."

"Uh—well, Dave and I have gotta get down to the gym. We'll see you."

Why should it hurt, when this guy is no one I'd want under any circumstances? But it does hurt. I won't let him see it.

"Come on, Dave," he yells from the sidewalk.

Dave sits down on the steps, near my legs. "You go on, Claudio," he says. "I didn't want to go to the gym anyway."

Claudio doesn't stick around long enough to argue. I watch him striding down the street. "Are you sure you don't want to go with him?" I ask Dave, and it's hard to keep the bitterness out of my voice.

"No," Dave says. "I was going to come sometime today and get acquainted. This seems like a good time, unless you're busy."

"Yes, she is," Julie says. "Dina promised to take me to see the lake."

"I'll walk with you," he says.

Julie stiffens, and I don't answer him. I don't know if I want his friendship or not. Is he going to be another Rob?

"Mrs. Cardenas told me you have Hodgkin's disease." Dave looks at me so intently I can't look away.

"You should have gone with Claudio."

"She also told me that you're an interesting person, a smart person. She said we'd find a lot to talk about."

"Did she ask you to come and see me?"

"Does that make a difference?"

"Shouldn't it?" I ask.

"Why?"

"Are you going to answer my question?"

"How do you like this game we're playing— answer a question with a question? Do you know you can be the winner if the other person goofs and makes a statement?"

I have to smile. "Are you crazy?"

He grins. "That's the spirit!" Then he slaps his hand over his mouth, and we both laugh.

The screen door squeals open, and Mrs. Cardenas comes out on the porch. "Hello, Dave," she says. "I'm glad you came by." And she adds, for my benefit, "Dave's a nice boy, *muy simpático*."

She may be right. I find that I'm glad Dave has come.

Mrs. Cardenas lowers herself into a chair and fans herself with her hand. "The hot weather is here for sure."

"I like it out here on the porch," I tell her. "And I like the sun. I've spent so long being cold."

"Did Julie tell you that some of my relatives are coming over tonight to meet both of you? Julie and I are going to make fudge brownies. All the kids like fudge brownies."

"Will you give out samples?" Dave asks.

"Come to the party," Mrs. Cardenas answers. "There's lots of room for everybody." She hoists herself out of the garden chair and says, "Come on, Julie. The oven's lit, and we should get busy with those brownies."

Julie's glance rapidly flickers between Dave and me. "I can't," she says. "We're going to walk to the lake."

I give her hand a reassuring squeeze. "We won't go to the lake without you. Have fun with the brownies."

"You'll be right here?"

"I won't leave the porch. I promise."

"Okay," Julie says reluctantly. She follows Mrs. Cardenas into the house, flashing Dave one last resentful glare.

"She's really hanging on to you," Dave says. "What's her problem?"

"She was in an accident. Both her parents were killed, and she has no other relatives. They put her in my room at the hospital, and I guess she needs someone to cling to for a little while."

"That's tough," he says, "on both of you."

Now's a good time to change the subject. "Claudio talked about the gym," I tell him. "Are you on some kind of team?"

"No," he says. "We were just going to goof around and see if there were enough guys there to get together a basketball game. Claudio's into all the sports, but I just tag along sometimes."

"What do you like to do?" I have to ask the next question. "Do you write?"

"No," he says, looking surprised. "My grades in English are good enough, but what I really like is science. I may go to med school after college. I don't know yet."

He's not another Rob. He doesn't write bad poetry. I lean forward, resting my arms on my knees. "Studying to be a doctor would be hard work. Will you specialize?"

"I don't know yet," he says. "It's the research that interests me the most."

So we talk about that for a while. I haven't talked to a guy my age for a long time, and I feel good about it until he says, "Tell me something about this Hodgkin's disease."

"What's there to tell? I don't even like to think about it."

"Well, I mean are you cured of it now?"

"No, I'm not!"

He turns toward me quickly, banging his right knee on the steps. He rubs his knee. "I didn't mean to make you mad."

"I'm not mad at you. I'm mad at—" Suddenly it's too much, and everything spills out. "We talked about what you want to be. Well, I was going to be an attorney. And now I'm not. My doctor says the percentages of people who survive the disease are getting higher all the time, but face it. There are some who don't survive."

"They let you out of the hospital. That must mean something."

"I'm what they call 'in remission.' That means I'm sort of hanging in space until the disease comes up and zaps me again."

"You're giving up."

"I'm facing facts."

"What you're doing is telling yourself that you're going to die."

There is a gasp behind me. I turn to see Julie standing in the open door, her face against the screen.

"Julie!" I say. "I didn't hear you!"

The door slams, and all I can see is the imprint of her stricken face.

"What a terrible way for her to find out!" I am on my feet, reaching for the door.

But Dave is beside me, and he grabs my arm. "Why don't you tell her that you've got a good chance, too?"

"Because I don't believe that I have."

"You don't know anything for sure. Sit down for a minute. Think this out."

I sit on the steps next to him, shaking my head, trying to remove the memory of Julie's face. Dave pulls a leaf from the ligustrum bush that crowds the edge of the steps and turns it over and over as though he's studying it.

"Look at it this way. Even if you were an attorney—a really good attorney—for ten years, or five years—" He stares right into my eyes. "Even if it was for only one year, Dina, you would have reached a goal, wouldn't you?"

I jump up. "I can't talk now. I've got to explain things to Julie."

"Want me to help?"

"No, thanks."

He stands on the lower step, squinting at me in the sunlight. "I'll be back."

"Are you sure you want to?"

He doesn't have time to answer. The windows rattle with Mrs. Cardenas's shriek. I stumble up the steps, banging through the pair of doors. Dave is right behind me.

Julie is standing in the middle of the kitchen. Blood is splattered on her clothes, the sink, and the floor.

"She must have tried to chop some more nuts!" Mrs. Cardenas cries. "I told her not to—the knife —she cut—oh! *¡Madre de Dios!* Could it be an artery? We got to stop the bleeding!"

I am at Julie's side in an instant. It's not an artery. I know that much from first aid. And I know my pressure points and what to do. Things are under control before my heart is. It's still popping around in my chest when I take a look at Julie's woebegone face. It has a good color.

"It looks as though she lost more blood than she did," I tell Mrs. Cardenas. "See—it's just a surface cut, and the bleeding has practically stopped. She won't even need stitches."

"Should we take her to the doctor?"

"We won't need to," I answer. "If you've got something to make a bandage with and an anti-septic I'll take care of it."

"In the medicine cabinet." Mrs. Cardenas hurries toward the bathroom.

"How did you know what to do?" Dave seems impressed.

"I teach— I used to teach a first-aid class."

Mrs. Cardenas returns with gauze pads and tape. "I thought I was watching. A big girl of nine. I told her not to touch the knife. Oh, *pobrecita niña*. I wasn't careful enough."

"You were careful, Mrs. Cardenas. Don't blame yourself. This was Julie's fault."

Mrs. Cardenas and Dave have an armful of paper towels and a pan of hot, soapy water, and are mopping the floor and cabinets.

Julie's gaze is steady, blinkless. "I just wanted to help chop some nuts."

"You were told not to touch the knife."

"I forgot. I wanted to help."

"You heard what I said to Dave. You were upset."

She nods. "I know. I was upset. That's why I wasn't careful. I tried to be careful, but I wasn't."

Mrs. Cardenas straightens with a grunt, one hand at her back. "You gave us a terrible scare."

"I'm sorry," Julie says. She holds her arm stiffly and examines the bandage.

Dave dries his hands on the seat of his jeans. "I'd better leave," he says. "But I'll be back."

"Tonight? For the brownies?" Mrs. Cardenas asks.

"Sure," he says.

I walk with him to the door, stepping out onto the porch.

"One question," he says in a low voice. "If someone is chopping nuts and the knife slips, they cut a finger or thumb. Right?"

"I know," I answer. "I wondered how she cut her arm instead."

The honeysuckle fragrance is strong in the hot noon sun. It's cloying and drowsy and makes a lie of the emotional upheaval we've just been through. For an instant I close my eyes. Then I look at Dave. "I'll talk to her," I say. "I've got to explain what she overheard."

He nods. "See you later."

I don't watch him leave. I go back into the house, to the hum of the air conditioner and the blasts of cooler air, but it's not that which makes me shiver.

Julie is sitting in one of the big deep red over-stuffed chairs. I sit across from her in a matching chair, feeling as though I'm in the mouth of a large, plush lion who is going to swallow me at any minute. I can hear Mrs. Cardenas on the phone again. She's speaking in Spanish, rapidly, excitedly.

"There's blood on your shirt," Julie says.

"I know, and on your clothes, too. In a few minutes we can change, and I'll wash them out."

"It was just an accident," Julie says.

"Let's talk about something else. About what you overheard."

"You're going to die, too."

"Julie, I don't know when. No one really knows when they're going to die. This disease I've got can stay in remission for years."

"For a long time?"

I begin to parrot what I've been told. "Dr. Cruz said that right now there's a good chance for a cure. In the future something may be discovered that will cure everyone who gets Hodgkin's. At some time the disease may be wiped out."

"The way you say it, I can tell you don't believe it," Julie says. "You don't care."

"What if I care too much and don't make it through college? Or hope too hard and don't make it through law school? What if I want to fall in love, but the disease comes back? It's that caring and wondering and hurting that I don't think I can handle." Am I talking to Julie or to myself?

"I don't want to be alone," she says.

"Oh, Julie, you aren't alone. I'm sorry you're upset about what I said. I didn't explain myself very well, I guess." Why did I expect a nine-year-old to understand all this?

She stares at me with those solemn eyes. "My father died," she says abruptly, startling me. "Sikes killed him. It was dark one night, and they fought and kept banging into the side of our mobile home. I was scared and I screamed, but my mother tried to make me be quiet. Somebody called the police, I think."

She is quiet, staring at something only she can see.

"Julie," I ask, "did Sikes threaten your father after they fought? Did he say he'd get even?"

Julie turns and looks at me. "Dina," she says, "there's something I want to show you."

"Now?"

"No," she says. "I'll tell you when."

CHAPTER 9

Mrs. Cardenas's party is a clustering of relatives, all sizes and ages and shapes. Mr. Cardenas is having as much fun as his wife. He argues politics with anyone who will listen, a strand of gray hair flopping on his forehead as his head punctuates his remarks.

"Dina," he says every time he passes me, "are you having a good time? Do you like the party?" His weathered cheeks are crinkled with laugh lines, and the black eyes that peer over the top of his out-of-shape wire-frame glasses are interested, eager.

"Most of the time," he confides to me in a voice that can be heard throughout the room, "I'd rather sleep in my chair than hear all these noisy relations, but sometimes it's a good thing for everyone to be together."

I meet Carmen and Dolores and many people whose names I can't remember. There are a number of children, but Julie clings to my side and doesn't attempt to talk to them.

Arturo, the policeman, is there. I am as curious to meet these relatives of Mrs. Cardenas as they are to meet me. Arturo shakes my hand and looks down at Julie. "*Muy bonita,*" he says. "She must be much like her mother."

"Come! Come get something to eat," Mrs. Cardenas shouts, pulling Arturo toward the kitchen.

Someone with a broad, red-lipstick smile shoves a loaded plate into my hands. There's a fragrance of spicy meat and flaky piecrust, and moist cake and buttery chocolate frosting. "Eat up! Enjoy the good food," she says. "I made the *empanadas,* which, between you and me, are a lot better than Carmen's."

Dave squeezes through the front door and searches the room until he sees me. Suddenly, surprisingly, I'm glad he's here. He works his way to my side and takes a piece of cake from my plate.

"Hi," he says. "I know you'd want me to help you eat that." He looks down at Julie. "Are you having a good time?" he asks.

She doesn't answer, so he adds, "Tomorrow I'd like to take you and Dina down to the river walk, Paseo del Rio. Have you ever been there?"

"No," Julie says.

"Would you like that?" Now he's looking at me.

"Yes, I'd like that very much," I tell him. "I was there once, a few years ago, and I'd like to see it again." I glance at the green circle on Julie's right hand. "It's where I bought that little jade ring."

Dave grabs the arm of a small boy who is wriggling past. "Ricky," he says, "take Julie to the other kids. She wants to play, too."

Ricky makes a face. "Do I gotta? We're going to play ball."

"Julie can play ball with you. Where's your sister, Estella? She's Julie's age."

"She's in the kitchen, stuffing her face."

"Okay. Take Julie and go find her. *¡Ahora!*"

Julie looks less eager to comply than Ricky does. "Where are you going?" she asks me in a voice filled with suspicion.

"I'm not going anywhere. I'm here enjoying the party. I think it's a good idea if you have fun with the other children."

She moves away, and once more I am myself.

I hold my plate out to Dave, and this time he takes a sandwich from it. Someone small dashes between us, stepping on my toes. "I seem to have a lot of foster relatives," I say.

"I think you've got a good deal," he answers, licking some cheese spread from his finger. "If I were picking a foster home, I'd check on the cooking first. Mrs. Cardenas is a good cook."

As though on cue Mrs. Cardenas makes her way

toward us. She is carrying a platter filled with some kind of little sausage buns. Dave takes one in each hand, and begins to eat them.

"I'm glad you came, Dave," she says. "This house is too full of people, and it's gonna make Dina tired. She met everybody, and now she needs to get out. Why don't you take her to a movie?"

I can't look at Dave. I'm so embarrassed I wish I was on the other side of the room.

"I was thinking about that," Dave says easily. "I like your relatives, Mrs. Cardenas, but you know I come to your parties just for the food."

She laughs loudly. "Then, get some punch and cake before you go."

"Wait a minute." It's time for me to break in. "I can't leave. I told Julie I'd be here."

"Why should Julie care if you and Dave go to a movie?"

"She wants me around. She's unsure of herself. She's—well, she's unsure of me."

Mrs. Cardenas gestures with the large platter, nearly spilling the contents. "Look at her. She's having a good time. Carmen's little girls are keeping her busy."

Dave nods. "I think it would be better for Julie if you didn't worry about her. Let her play with the kids her age."

Guilt slides away like a shadow at noon. They're right. And I need to be away from Julie. "You talked me into it," I tell them.

"I'll go home and get my father's car and the

movie listings in the newspaper while you get ready," Dave says.

He makes his way out of the house. Julie looks up, watches him leave, then goes back to her new friends.

The noise level is rising. It's beginning to bother me. So I get my handbag and slip out to the front porch. An evening breeze has come up, and a wisp of hair tickles my face.

My hair is getting longer! I reach up to touch it in wonder. My hair is growing!

Dave pulls the car to a stop in the street. He gets out and comes toward me, but I run to meet him.

"You look happy," he says. "Are you that glad to leave the party?"

"My hair is growing!" I tell him. It sounds so silly that we both laugh. But he puts a hand to my head and strokes the short curls.

"I like your hair. It's so soft. It's soft like—well—like the belly of a duck."

It's so ludicrous that we laugh as though we'll never stop. He's holding my shoulders, and I'm warm with the happy chatter coming from inside the house and the night burst of honeysuckle perfume and the sharp-tipped moon.

Dave opens the car door for me, and I slide across to the middle of the seat. It's not until after he edges the car away from the curb that I realize his closeness, the warmth of his body next to mine. What am I doing? Slowly, carefully, I move a few inches away.

Dave gives me a quick glance, a grin. "Where are you going?" he asks.

"I was crowding you."

"Oh, no, you weren't." When I don't answer, he says, "For a few minutes you were relaxed and having a good time. Now you're sitting all by yourself with your hands clenched in your lap. What's the matter?"

"Nothing," I answer quickly. "I just didn't want you to think—I mean, this isn't exactly a date."

"Why isn't it?"

"Because—" I shrug. "Look, Dave, there was a guy named Rob. We were dating, and I thought he felt about me the way I felt about him. Except that after I came to the hospital, I never heard from him again. He's dating someone else. And I don't blame him. I just don't want to be hurt like that again."

"There was a girl named Arlene," he says. That's all.

After a minute I turn to him. "What is that supposed to mean?"

"It means that you're not the only one who's been hurt. My mom said it's a part of growing up."

I sigh. "I suppose she called it 'puppy love'?"

"No. She said it's real and it's painful, but relationships either grow into something lasting and serious, or they break up, and at our age they usually break up. Most of the time someone's left with a lot of unhappiness to handle."

"Then it's better to protect yourself from getting hurt."

He smiles. "That's exactly what I told her, and she said that people who are afraid of being hurt can never find out how wonderful love can be."

"So you take your chances?"

"Isn't it worth it?"

"I don't know. I'll have to think about it." I settle back against the seat feeling more comfortable about the evening. It's easy to talk to Dave. I have to admit to myself that I like being with him.

During the movie I glance sideways at Dave. In the flickering light with his tortoiseshell glasses he reminds me again of Rob. Rob who? Rob Who-cares-about-Rob? I giggle, and Dave turns toward me.

"It's a funny movie," I whisper.

On the way home we talk about a lot of things, but not about me and not about Julie. I tell him about my high school and how Holley Jo and I, not knowing any better, tried out for the cheerleader squad against all those juniors and seniors and didn't get a single vote but got invited to the football dance. And he tells me about his high school and how Claudio ran last year for Student Council and made stacks of posters with his picture on them and even plastered them inside all the girls' lavatories at school. And I tell him that speaking of posters, I won an honorable-mention prize for a poster I made in a good-nutrition contest. And he tells me that speaking of good nutrition, there's a mom-and-pop place in San Antonio that makes the best *burritos de guisada* in the world.

For a few hours I've forgotten who I am. But as we go up the walk to Mrs. Cardenas's house, there is Julie, sitting on the top step of the porch, looking lost in someone's hand-me-down pajamas.

"What are you doing out here?" I ask her.

"It's all right. Mrs. Cardenas hasn't gone to bed yet."

"I'll help her clean up."

"No. Everybody helped. It's all clean. She's watching a movie on TV. She says she's wound up and has to run down."

Dave sits on the step next to her, and I sit on the other side. She turns, so that her back is toward Dave and says to me accusingly, "You told me you'd be at the party."

"I know, but Mrs. Cardenas suggested that we go to a movie."

"I would have gone with you."

"You were playing with your friends."

"They're not my friends. Just some kids."

"I saw you. You were having fun."

"I wanted to go with you."

"You'll be going with us tomorrow," Dave says. "Let's talk about that. We can walk along the river, under the bridges that are streets. And there's an ice cream shop you'll like."

Julie's back is stiff, but she's listening. "There's a theater out of doors, with the seats on one side of the river and the stage on the other, and some restaurants where you can sit outside and watch the boats go by."

"What kind of boats?" She turns toward him just a little.

"They're flat-bottomed boats that the tourists ride on. But they're not as much fun as the paddle-boats that are on the part of the river that runs through Brackenridge Park."

"By the zoo," I add.

"There's a zoo?" Now she is really interested.

"It's in a different part of the city, but we'll go there sometime, too," Dave says.

I can't help but yawn. The excitement that has kept me going begins to dissipate, and I feel like a portable cassette with its battery level sliding downward.

Dave is smiling at me, over Julie's head. "Good night," he says. "I'll pick you both up tomorrow afternoon around two."

Julie stands and takes one of my hands, helping me to my feet. "Good-bye," she says formally.

"Good night," he answers.

Julie tugs me into the house, but I turn to watch him drive away.

We say good night to Mrs. Cardenas. Her eyes glitter, reflecting the blue and white light from the television screen. "Julie, what are you doing out of bed?" she asks, but without waiting for an answer, she says to me, "Did you have a good time with Dave?"

"Yes. It was fun."

"He's a nice boy." She looks as pleased as if she had put him together with her own hands. "Oh, what a nice evening!" she says, and turns back to watch Cary Grant murmur something clever to Sophia Loren. Down the hall I can hear the snuffles and sputters as Mr. Cardenas dreams and snores.

I wish I could talk to Holley Jo. I would love to tell her about Dave. I will. Right now, before the evening has begun to blur, I'll write her a letter. If I can't talk to her before we fall asleep, then I'll write my thoughts. Once in the bedroom, I put on my nightgown and begin to look through the drawer for my box of stationery.

"What are you doing?" Julie asks. She pokes her head out from under the blanket.

"I'm looking for my stationery."

"What for? You aren't going to write a letter in the middle of the night."

"Oh, yes, I am." I turn to look at her. "Did you see my box of stationery? It's pink, and it has some pink and white envelopes and paper in it and a bundle of my letters from Holley Jo and some other friends."

"No."

"You helped pack my things, and you put them away. You must have seen the box. I don't own that much."

"Maybe it got left accidentally at the hospital."

She is staring straight into my eyes, and I know she's lying. For an instant I am so furious with this child that I want to scream at her, but I clench my fists and try to think. If she deliberately left the box at the hospital, they'll find it and keep it for me. And if she didn't, then it's probably somewhere here in this room. And if she threw it out, there hasn't been a trash pickup, so it would still be in the trash can. I can search for it tomorrow. Why would she do a thing like this? I know she's jealous of Dave. Is she even jealous of Holley Jo and my past life?

Back to the check of drawers.

"Hey! That's my drawer!" She jumps out of bed and runs to my side. But I have found my stationery box under her clothes, and I pull it out, holding it over her head.

She pushes the drawer shut, then turns and marches back to her bed as though her feelings had been deeply hurt. "I tried to put everything away by myself," she says. "If I got something in the wrong drawer, it's not my fault."

"Why did you do this?"

"Do what?" Her gaze is clear blue.

There's no point in pursuing it. "I'm going to write a letter. If the light bothers you, just roll toward the wall. It won't take long." I know my voice sounds colder than I mean it to be, but I can't help it.

The mood is broken. I sit cross-legged at the center of the sagging mattress, the box balanced on my lap, a sheet of paper on it. *Dear Holley Jo.* I look at the words, the only words on the paper.

I can't write. I'm even having trouble thinking
straight. There's so much I want to write you,
Holley Jo, and I can't. I want to tell you about
Dave, but I keep looking over at the other bed, and
there is Julie, lying on her back, staring straight
ahead without blinking. It makes me blink just to
think of someone not blinking. It makes my eyes
feel itchy and start to water. Holley Jo, there is a
lot I don't understand about Julie. She's had some
awful things happen to her, and maybe that's the
problem. What problem? I don't know. I don't
understand what I'm thinking, so how can I write
it? I only wanted to tell you about this guy, Dave,
but all those other thoughts have me too mixed up
to write. I look again at the words I've written:
Dear Holley Jo. Not much of a letter.

I slip the paper and pen inside the box, lean down
and put it on the floor. "Don't ever touch this box
again," I tell Julie.

Tears are running in little streaks into her hair
and her ears. She hasn't made a sound. I didn't
realize she was crying. "What I'm trying to say,
Julie, is that the letters in this box mean a lot to me,
and I don't want anything to happen to them. You
understand, don't you?"

Julie gives a loud snuffle and her eyes close. "I
told you I just got mixed up when I tried to put
everything away. It wasn't my fault, and you didn't
even say you were sorry."

The yellow lamp is harsh, and the fading bruises
on her arms are still there—blotches that remind

me how much she is hurting. "All right, Julie. I'm sorry there was a misunderstanding. I'm going to turn out the light now, so we can sleep."

"Good night," she says.

In the morning Mrs. Cardenas serves another big breakfast. Then she announces it's time to get ready for Mass. "Nobody has to go," she says. "But it would be nice. After all, it is the Lord's day, and you don't have to be Catholic to go to Mass."

"She makes everybody go to Mass," Mr. Cardenas says.

His wife ignores him. "In a family it's a good thing when everybody goes to church together. You see, I'm not telling you to go. I'm just saying it would be nice." She cocks her head like a fat little robin as she looks at me. "Dina, did you ever go to Mass in a Catholic church?"

"No."

"Well then," she says, "you don't know what it's like, how beautiful it is, and you won't know unless you go."

How do I explain to her that I'm blank inside, that I tried to pray and I couldn't? "Please," I say. "I'm not ready yet. Not now."

She gives me a long look, then nods. "Okay. Not just yet. How about you, Julie? Want to come with me?"

"I want to stay with Dina," Julie says.

Mrs. Cardenas sighs. "Then it's up to you and me, Carlos."

He leans on the table and pushes himself upward

from his chair. The wood creaks, and he says, "That's my knees complaining they're getting too stiff to kneel."

"Going to church is good for stiff knees."

"She is trying to make me holy," he says to me.

"You're much closer than you used to be," she says.

"Maybe it's not going to church that's doing it. Maybe it's old age."

"Hurry up, old man," she tells him.

"I'll take care of the kitchen," I say. I carry the plates nearest me to the sink and rinse off the runny yellow egg yolk that paints the rims.

Julie comes to the sink, too, and nudges me out of the way. "I said I'd do the breakfast dishes."

"We can do them together, and make the beds, and then read the comics in the newspaper."

"You're supposed to rest."

"I just got up. I'm not the least bit tired." I smile at her. "Come on, Julie. Let's work together."

"All right," she says, putting the dishes she is holding into the sink. "And then you can write your letter."

But the letter doesn't get written. In just an hour Mr. and Mrs. Cardenas return, and there are preparations for dinner and everything anyone said at the party to retell in detail. Mrs. Cardenas is still hung over with happiness.

Dave comes at two, just as he had promised, and we climb into his father's car. Somehow Julie ends up between us.

"*Hola, señorita,*" he tells her.

"Is that Spanish?" she asks.

"Yes. Wouldn't you feel less crowded in the backseat?"

"No," she says, and she folds her hands primly in her lap.

Dave smiles at me over Julie's head, and I feel a rush of joy in this special day that belongs to me.

Dave has a nice smile and a nice profile. I memorize it with quick, secret glances as we drive through the older part of the city and the downtown area. Finally we park in a wide lot near the Hilton Hotel.

"The river is to our right, but we're going to La Villita first," Dave says. "A glass blower there makes little animals. I think Julie would like one."

Julie perks up. She chatters about a glass blower she saw at the beach once when her father took her, as we cross the street and head into a narrow passageway paved with cobblestones.

Dave is telling us about the history of this early center in San Antonio, but I am watching the people and the shops. The area is filled with tourists.

"The glassblower first," Julie says, as I stop to look at a pottery display in a nearby window. Someone takes my hand, but it's not Julie. The fingers are long and firm, and I like the feel of them.

I see that Dave has Julie by his other hand. He has moved between us. Across the way a tall, stocky man with dark hair is watching the three of us, and

I automatically smile at him. This is a day for smiles.

If he smiles back, I don't notice because Dave is saying, "Right in here, Julie," and fishing some change from his pocket to pay the ten cents admission.

We edge past some plump women who are leaving the store, gingerly carrying well-wrapped purchases, and enter an ice-and-diamond-spangled world. There are blown glass figurines of all sizes and shapes lining the walls and hanging from the ceiling. Ships in full sail, ballerinas, skittish horses, leaping porpoises—

"This is fantastic!" I tell Dave.

Julie adds, "Oh! Look at the merry-go-round!"

"Tell you what, Julie," Dave says. "I'd like to buy you anything in the store, but I haven't got that much money. Over on this tray are a lot of little animals, and I can afford one of those for you. Take your pick."

Julie is delighted. She chooses, changes her mind, and chooses again until she has decided on a small, pink dog. "I never had a dog," she says.

Dave has picked something else. He pays for the purchases and puts mine in my hand. "A duck," he says. "A very soft-bellied duck."

We leave the store laughing in our own world, not noticing that Julie has stopped on the bottom step, until we nearly stumble over her.

"Watch it!" Dave says, catching his footing and grabbing my arm.

"Sikes!" Julie whispers, and she clutches my skirt. "That man looking in the window, with his back to us, is Sikes!"

Before I can react, she begins to run into the crowd, back toward the street. "Dave!" I cry. "Catch her!"

A policeman is standing on the next level. Should I yell for help? No. My mind is trying to think while my feet are running toward him.

He turns. "What's the matter?"

My words gulp and gasp and spill into each other. "There's a man. His name is Sikes. Please come with me."

I lead, and he follows quickly. It isn't far. The shop is here—no, there. At the window. But he's gone.

"Oh, no! He was a big man. Tall, with dark hair. His back was toward us. He must have seen me run to you for help. He's—"

The door of the shop opens, and a woman comes out, her wide-brimmed straw hat flopping at every step. The man follows her. It's the same man who had been watching us earlier.

"It was hot in the sun," he complains. "I thought you were never going to make up your mind."

"That's him," I tell the policeman. I don't have to go toward him. He and the woman walk right into our path.

"Just a minute, please," the policeman says, and they stop. The policeman looks at me.

I glance wildly around for Dave and Julie, but

they aren't in sight. "I—there's a little girl with us. She—well, she was afraid of this man. She said his name was Sikes. William Sikes."

"For goodness' sakes!" the woman says. She squints at us and retreats behind an overlarge pair of sunglasses. "That's not our name. It isn't even close."

"I'll show you my identification," the man tells the policeman. He pulls out a wallet, and the policeman studies it. I wish I were any place in the world except right here.

"Dina!" I am so glad to hear Dave's voice. He comes through the crowd, pulling Julie after him. She looks at me as though I had betrayed her, and she's trembling. "I don't want to see him, Dina!"

I take her other hand. "Look, Julie. This is the man you ran from."

She stares at him and shakes her head. "He isn't Sikes."

"He's the man who was looking in the window. You just saw his back. You made a mistake."

Other people have stopped to watch the scene. I feel like a fool, trying to apologize, to explain. There is really nothing I can explain. I wish the man and his wife would help me, but they're annoyed. They walk away.

The policeman shrugs and goes back to the spot where I had found him. He isn't curious, and I'm thankful for that. How do I explain someone like Sikes?

Dave has a hand on my shoulder. "Calm down,"

he says. "Julie just made a mistake. No one got hurt."

"I want to go home," Julie says.

"But we haven't been to the river yet. And whoever you thought this guy was, he wasn't." Dave pauses. "Does that make sense?"

"I know that man wasn't Sikes," Julie says, as she stares at the clusters of people who are strolling past us. Her fingers grip my hand so tightly it's painful.

"I wasn't looking at that man," Julie adds. "I was looking at Sikes."

CHAPTER 10

"Who is Sikes?" Dave asks me later, so I tell him Julie's story.

"That's weird," he says. He leans back on the thick pad of grass under Mrs. Cardenas's crape myrtle tree. The tree is dotted with hard little gray-green balls that in a few weeks will relax and become fragile pink flowers.

"Her story is possible," I tell him. "Mrs. Cardenas thinks Julie's parents were running from something or someone. I wonder if they were running from Sikes."

"Do you think he's following Julie? Or does she just imagine that she sees him?"

I pull at a broad strand of grass and smooth it between my fingers. "Dave, I've even wondered if Sikes was a real person. But he must be. The things she's told me she couldn't make up. And she does have those marks on her back and bruises on her arms."

"Maybe they came from her father."

"I doubt it. She adores her father. She told me she looks just like him." I watch a bee who is investigating my toes. I pull my foot back, and he shoots off in a straight line. "That's odd."

Dave rolls over on one elbow. "It's odd that she looks like her father?"

"No. I just thought of something Arturo said. At the party he mentioned that Julie was a pretty little girl. Then he said she must look like her mother."

"It was a compliment."

"I don't think so. He's a policeman. Maybe he saw the driver's license description of her father. Or maybe it's the Texas kind that has a picture on it, and he knows what her father looks like."

"Remind me to show you the picture on my driver's license. No. Remind me not to. I look like I'm planning to rob the savings and loan company. All I need is a number under my chin."

"I'll show you my license. I've got a big, silly grin that scrunches up my eyes. If a policeman ever stopped me and looked at my license, he'd never recognize me unless I made the same face."

It's a lazy afternoon. The scene at La Villita seems out of place. Wrong movie. Wrong actors. I've forgotten something.

"Dave, I didn't remember to thank you for going after Julie."

"She's a fast one," Dave says. "Scared me to death when she ran out in the traffic before I could reach her. She just missed being hit by a car. It's surprising she wasn't."

Cold, cold, cold. Sitting in the sun with shivers up my back and through my shoulders and into my neck. There is something here I don't understand. A needle of cold pricks me, frightens me. Dave begins talking about his job, and I'm distracted. Tomorrow I'll call Dr. Lynn. I need to talk to her. All I have is pieces, and I need her to help put them together.

"So frying fish and french fries gets kind of boring after a while, but the job pays okay, and it's fine for summer."

I realize Dave is talking, but it's hard to pay attention.

What do I tell her? About Julie cutting her arm? But it was an accident. About Julie running into traffic? But she was running away from someone she thought was Sikes.

I try to look interested as Dave says, "And you can sure get sick of that fish smell. We get all we can eat, but you can only eat so much fish, and you start dreaming it's a pizza."

What's happening to Julie doesn't make sense. It sounds crazy. She's just a little girl. With problems.

"Obviously the story of my career as a fryer of

fish has you stunned into speechlessness," Dave says.

I tuck away the problems, pulling myself back to the here and now, back to Dave. "I was just trying to visualize the story of your job as a TV miniseries. Sort of like cooked *Jaws*."

I feel at ease with Dave, and he likes to be with me. I know he does. But the afternoon turns warm again, and it's over too soon. Reluctantly I say good-bye to Dave and go into the house. Mrs. Cardenas is chopping cucumbers and tomatoes for a salad, so I set the table.

Mr. Cardenas tosses down the comic section of the *Express-News*.

"There's nothing funny in here today," he says.

"You read those comics three times at least," his wife says. "If they're not funny, why read them?"

"I keep looking."

The house is very quiet. "Where's Julie?" I ask. I'm glad I had a break from her, but now guilt is moving in again.

"Oh, she's back in the bedroom. Probably still playing with that little glass dog," Mrs. Cardenas says. "She sure likes that little dog. That was nice of Dave to buy those things for you. Didn't I tell you he was a nice boy?"

Yes, he's very nice, and the little duck is nice, and I want to see it and touch it again. "I'll go back to the bedroom and talk to Julie," I tell them. "She may want some company."

As I enter the bedroom, Julie stares up at me.

There is a strong message of fear. She is hunched in a little ball in the middle of her bed, and she holds out a closed fist.

"I want you to have my dog," she says.

Pink glass shines through her fingers.

"No," I tell her. "That's a gift to you from Dave. He wouldn't want you to give it away."

"I want to give it to you, because I broke your little duck."

"Oh, no, Julie! No!" I glance at the top of the chest of drawers, where I had put it, but it isn't there. "What were you doing with it?"

"I know. It was yours, and I should have left it alone."

"Where is it? How did you break it?"

She climbs from the bed and carefully picks up a tissue which is wadded around something. I hold out my hand, and she places the tissue in it.

"I dropped it. Please don't be mad at me. I was just looking at it, and I dropped it."

I stare at the crushed pieces of yellow glass lying on the tissue in my hand. "Tell me the truth, Julie."

"I am! I dropped it."

"To smash it like this you must have stepped on it."

"Oh. Maybe I did when I was trying to pick it up."

I meet her gaze, so steady, so innocent. She had to do this on purpose. Because Dave gave it to me?

Facing her, I sit on the edge of my bed. She is

so small, so thin, so young for her nine years. "I think if we have an honest talk with each other, it will help," I tell her. "Something is bothering you, and something is bothering me. Talk to me. Tell me why you did this."

She looks at me for a long time, and I hope she is weighing what I've said.

"Julie, do you think I'm spending too much time with Dave and not enough with you?"

She shakes her head.

"People have many friends. At the home I spent a lot of time with Holley Jo, but I had other friends, too. And I taught swimming lessons in the summer, while Holley Jo took advanced French in summer school. And sometimes she went out on a date, and I stayed home. Sometimes it worked the other way. We didn't have to be with each other the entire time. Do you understand?"

Her mind has shifted, and I can see the change. "I know what's bothering you," she suddenly says. "You don't like being sick and waiting to find out if you're going to die."

I can't help sighing. "I am trying to talk about you. The way you've been behaving is one of the things that is bothering me."

Does she smile? It was just a flicker. A strange, little smile. "Don't worry," she says. "Everything's going to be all right."

I can't get through to her. I don't know how. Carefully, I wrap the shards of yellow glass in the tissue and tuck it in the right-hand corner of my top drawer. When I get the chance, I'm going to call Dr. Lynn.

In the morning Mrs. Cardenas leans across the breakfast table and says, "Dina, you told me you could drive and run errands for me. You got a driver's license?"

"Yes. I'll show it to you."

"That's okay. I believe you." She plops back in her chair and says, "Carlos is such a bad driver he takes the bus to work. And I don't like to drive. Too many crazy drivers who want to put their cars in the same spot my car is in."

"I'll take you anywhere you want to go," I say. "I'm a good driver."

"*Muy bien,*" she says. "Today I got some errands for you."

"I want to go, too," Julie says.

"Sure," Mrs. Cardenas says. "This one place you're going to, a shoe repair shop—Oh, how that man wears down the heels on his shoes!—is right next to a nice little ice cream store. I'll give you some money to have ice cream cones."

"Thank you," I say, and Julie repeats it like a small echo.

"You'd better give me some directions," I add. "I'm not familiar with San Antonio."

Julie clears the table while Mrs. Cardenas draws red dots on a gas station map of the city. "Here's where we are, and here's the shoe repair shop. It's in a big shopping mall over near the Loop. I'm going to give you a grocery list, and you may as well get the things at that store in the mall because they got a good buy on eggs and a half-price on tomato juice."

She's busy writing lists, and I'm studying the map. The city isn't that big, and map reading isn't hard. In fact, I like it.

Julie is next to me. Her finger points to I-10. "This is the freeway that goes to the hospital," she says.

"You're a good map reader," I tell her.

"I know," she answers.

Finally we are loaded with a list; a paper bag with a pair of shoes in it; Mr. Cardenas's suit, which has to go to the dry cleaners; and some money for the grocery store.

"Once around the block until you're used to the car," Mrs. Cardenas says, piling into the front seat with us, squashing Julie up against me.

Mrs. Cardenas's car is like the old blue station wagon. It takes the same gentle hand to keep from bucking. This beautiful model comes complete with jumps and stalls. I know its tricks, so by the time we get down the hill to Woodlawn Drive, I've got the feel of the car. Right turn, right turn, up the hill, and right turn again.

"This house with the blue trim—it's where Dave Lewis and his family live," Mrs. Cardenas says smugly, adding, "Nice boy, Dave."

I wonder what time Dave goes to work. He didn't say when he'd come over.

The car pulls to a smooth stop in front of Mrs. Cardenas's house, and she beams. "You're a good driver, Dina. Have fun, and take your time. There's no hurry."

She struggles from the car and onto the curb, panting a little. "Dr. Cruz says I gotta lose weight. Sometimes I think he's right."

She shuts the door, waves, and I head down to Woodlawn again. Julie scoots over and watches our progress intently. She asks questions about the zoo, so I fill time telling her how kids under twelve can ride on the elephant, and how the little train goes all around the park.

She sits on the edge of her seat, resting her arms on the dashboard and her chin on her arms. As we pull into the large shopping area, she says, "I've been here before."

"Did you live near here?" I drop the keys into my handbag.

"Yes." She swings toward me and clutches my arm. "Dina, remember I said there was something I wanted to show you? Well, now it's time."

"We have some errands to do."

"After the errands." She climbs out of the car as though everything had been settled.

Cleaners, first, then shoe repair shop. "How about that ice cream cone now?" I ask her.

"I don't want an ice cream cone."

Heat rises from the expanse of cement. "I think ice cream would make us feel a lot cooler."

"Let's go to the grocery store."

"Why are you in such a hurry?"

"I'm not in a hurry," Julie says. "I just know what I want to do."

"What is it you want to do?"

"I want to go where I used to live." She's marching down the pavement, turning into the super-market. The huge glass doors swing wide as we approach and close behind us with a smack.

I drag a cart from its stack and pull out the shopping list. "Julie, you told Detective Mac-Garvey that you didn't know where you lived."

"I don't remember the address, but I know how to get there."

"You could have told him that."

"I didn't want to. It wasn't time to go there."

"And it is now?"

"Yes," she says. "Now it's time."

"Why don't we call Detective MacGarvey? He could go with us."

"No!"

"Okay," I say. "Don't get so upset."

The list isn't long, so soon we are back in the car, the bags tucked on the floor behind the front seat.

"I'll tell you how to get there," she says. She sits upright, clutching the dashboard, staring out the windshield. "Turn down this street, next to the freeway, and keep going until I tell you to turn."

Freeway traffic zooms past, up on a raised level,

a purring, swishing, rattling roar. I'm not in that traffic, but it's invaded my life, and for a moment I wish for the quiet roads of the hill country.

"Here," she says. "Turn here. Wait! Not so fast! Pull in right here and park."

I turn off the ignition and stare at the dirty white stucco building in front of us. Curls of paint are peeling from the brown trim at the windows, and the asphalt shingles on the roof are streaked and stained. Occasional outside stairways break the flat monotony, and down at the far end is a sign with an arrow: MANAGER.

Julie is already out of the car, so I join her, carefully locking the doors because of those bags of food inside. I start toward the manager's office, but Julie says, "No! This way!"

"Don't we need to talk to the manager?"

She shakes her head. "Come on."

I follow her around the side and to the back, where sagging carports stretch to the end of the unit. "Just where are we going?" I ask.

"To our apartment."

"But we'll have to ask the manager."

"No. We paid by the week. The time isn't up yet."

"You were leaving the city."

"We always do it that way. Sooner or later the manager finds the keys in our mailboxes. That way there aren't any questions about where we're going or forwarding addresses or stuff like that."

"Why, Julie?"

For a moment she looks puzzled, but she simply shrugs. "It's this one, downstairs."

She stoops at the door and fishes through a crack around the sill, coming up with a key. "I always hide my key," she says, "because sometimes Nancy goes out, and I'm outside and can't get in."

"Julie, are you sure we should go inside?"

But the door is open, and she has disappeared into the dimness. I follow her, carefully closing the door, feeling creepy in this dingy apartment with its smell of stale cigarette smoke and bacon grease, with its dusty beige drapes drawn against the sun.

Where is Julie? There's a small hallway leading off one end of the living room. Two bedrooms, but sounds are coming from the one on the right. I enter in time to see her backing out of the closet.

"It's here! I knew it would be!" She holds up a square, metal can, the kind cookies sometimes come in. It's scratched and dented, and the Christmas poinsettias on the cover are faded. She puts it on the one twin bed.

"What's inside?"

"Something I want to show you." She pries off the lid, holding it as a shield so that I can't see into the box. In a moment she has found what she wants. It's a snapshot. She studies it, then hands it to me.

The picture is that of a man who is smiling, and I see Julie's face. His nose is long and narrow, eyes wide and blue. He's standing on a bridge, and a strand of pale, thin hair is blowing across his fore-head.

"Is this your father?" I ask.

"We look alike," she tells me.

"You certainly do. Is there a picture of your mother in the box, too?"

Solemnly she takes the snapshot from me and carefully puts it back. She snaps the lid of the can shut and hugs it to her chest.

"Now we can go," she says.

"Julie, are there other things in the apartment that belong to your family?"

"No," she says.

"I think I'd better look around." I open a drawer of the nearby chest, but it's empty.

"I told you. They took everything except my treasure box."

"Why didn't they take that, too?"

"They decided to leave while I was at the playground. There's a little playground two blocks down that street out in front. And they just picked me up and said we were moving. Nancy had packed everything. I told them they had left my box, but they wouldn't go back." Her voice is rising, and there is such anger in her face that it frightens me.

"Why would they leave this—this treasure box?"

"Because I hid it. Everywhere we go I hide it, so no one will find it except me. There's always some-place. This closet has some boards loose on the floor. I hid it under the boards."

She is so intent she must be telling the truth, but

she has lied to me before. I can't be sure. I walk into the other bedroom. The bed is unmade. A pair of man's shoes are on the floor, a shirt draped over the small chair, cigarettes and matches on the chest. I open the top drawer. It's stuffed with men's underwear, some papers, rolled socks in a heap of disorder.

"Julie! Look at all this! Your parents didn't pack everything. There may be something here that will help Detective MacGarvey."

I flip through the papers. A credit card. A photograph. I pull them out. "George Washburn?" The photo is of a smiling family. They're black. "Julie, what is all this?"

She shrugs. "Maybe we just paid for one week. I forget. Someone else must live here now."

CHAPTER

11

I shove things back into the drawer as though they are crawly, alive, and biting. "Let's get out of here! We could be arrested for breaking into someone's apartment!"

"We didn't break in. I've got the key."

"Give it to me!"

I grab it from her fingers and run into the living room. I can hear footsteps across the walkway in front of the apartments. I hope whoever is out there is not coming in this apartment!

The footsteps stop. Julie comes up beside me. "Shhh," I whisper, and clutch her arm.

"Ouch!" she says.

I am frozen into the minute, which goes on and on. The footsteps move down the walk. I think I'm breathing. I think I'm moving across the room. The key. Where am I going to put the key? If Mr. Washburn finds it, he'll know someone was in the apartment.

There's a small table with a drawer in it. It rattles as I open it. The table isn't shaking. I am. There's nothing in the drawer except a phone book, so I drop the key in beside it and close the drawer.

No! The footsteps are returning!

I tug Julie out the back door, not even looking to see if anyone is outside. We're the only ones in this parking area.

"You're pulling my arm!"

"I'm sorry. I'm trying to make you hurry."

"Why?"

"Because we have to get away from this place. We have no business here."

"You sound like Nancy."

Here is the car. I can't find the keys. They're in my handbag somewhere. What happened to the person on the walk? No one is around now. Is someone watching us from one of the windows? The keys!

"Get in, Julie. Lock your door."

I'm still trembling as we drive away. It occurs to me, as we double back to the shopping center, that I haven't noted the name of the apartments, the name of the street, or the address.

"Now let's go home," she says calmly.

"That's where we're going."

"Why are you mad at me?"

"I'm not mad. I was just scared." Suddenly I

remember something she said. "Why did you tell me that I sounded like your mother?"

"Because she'd rush around and get excited when we had to leave."

"Did you always leave places in such a hurry?"

"Not all the time, but sometimes."

"Do you know why?"

"No."

"But you're a smart little girl, Julie. You must have figured something out. Was someone chasing your family?"

"Sometimes."

"Was it Sikes?"

"I hate Sikes. I wish he'd go away. He's mad because I didn't die, too."

Back to the beginning. "Why, why, why?"

"Don't yell at me."

This is no time to try to talk to her. I've got to watch the traffic. I must calm down. Take a long slow deep breath. Calmly, calmly, nothing matters now. Watch the traffic. Home again, home again, jiggity jog. What am I doing in this car with this child, playing this crazy game?

"I've got some other things in my treasure box to show you, but it's not time now."

"No, it's not. Not while I'm driving."

"I'll tell you when it's time."

"Good." I remember there's a radio in the car, and I turn it on. Country western. Familiar stuff. It eases me back to Mrs. Cardenas's house. I leave the car in the driveway.

"Don't tell Mrs. Cardenas about my treasure box," Julie says.

Mrs. Cardenas? I suppose it doesn't matter if she knows or not. It's Dr. Lynn I need to talk to.

"It has to be my secret for a while," Julie adds.

"Okay. I won't tell her."

I carry in one sack of groceries, and Mrs. Cardenas goes out for the other. Julie slips into the house like a small ghost. Mrs. Cardenas doesn't see her.

"Where's Julie?"

"She came in while you were going out." I hand her the sales slip and the change and put a head of lettuce in the refrigerator.

"Here I am," Julie says. Sweet smile. No sign of her treasure box. How did she do that so fast?

"Dave called. He said there's something he has to tell you, Dina. He's going to come over tonight after work, about eight o'clock."

"Is that too late? Will it bother Mr. Cardenas?"

"Nothing bothers Carlos, not even his own snoring. Dave said it was important."

It dawns on me that I don't have the number of the hospital. There must be a phone book around here. Where have I seen one? I remember the phone book in the dresser in George Washburn's apartment, and I shudder.

Mrs. Cardenas stops, a carton of milk in her hands, and studies me. "Are you cold, Dina? On such a warm day?

"Cold? Oh, no. I'm fine."

"You've been looking a lot better. I said to Carlos, 'There's been a big difference since she's been out in the sun and has more color in her face.' "

Julie is studying me, too. Don't worry. I won't give away your secret to Mrs. Cardenas. To me a promise is something to keep.

"What can I do to help you?" I ask Mrs. Cardenas.

"*Nada más.*" She shakes her head. "There are some books in the living room bookcase. Maybe you'll find something in there that you'd like to read. Carlos and I aren't much for reading, but we got our boys some books while they were home and in school."

Bookcase? I wonder if that's where she keeps the telephone book. It will give me an excuse to look.

She shuts the refrigerator door and says, "I almost forgot to tell you. My sister-in-law, Angie, is taking me shopping with her in a little while. She's going to buy some material to sew new drapes for their den, and she can't make up her mind. She can never make up her mind about anything. Always has to have somebody help her. This time it's me."

"Would you like me to drive you?"

"No, no. She has a car. She drives like her head is somewhere else, but I pray a lot, and we don't run into anybody. I just want you girls to know that I'll be gone for a couple of hours. You'll be all right, won't you? The doctors said I don't have to be with you every minute."

"We'll be fine," I tell her.

"Help yourself to whatever you want for lunch. There are still some of Carmen's *empanadas* in the refrigerator.

I sit on the floor in front of the built-in book-case. On the lower shelf, in a brown vinyl cover to make it look acceptable in the living room, is what I'm searching for—the phone book.

Mrs. Cardenas and Julie are chatting in the kitchen. I quickly look up the number of the hospital. I should have thought. No pencil or paper. I'll memorize it. I go over and over the number in my mind as I slide the phone book back into its place.

"Why are you just staring at those books?"

I jump. "Julie! I didn't hear you come up behind me."

"You're just staring at those books. Are you going to read one of them?"

I reach up and pull down *Tom Sawyer*. "Here's one you'd like. I could read it to you." The idea surprises me, even as I say the words. But it's a good idea. Sharing a book might make Julie more open with me. Maybe we can talk more about the things that have happened to her.

"That doesn't look like a book for children. It looks like those other books."

There aren't many books in the case, and most of them have the same inexpensive binding. Part of a set: Alcott, Twain, Dickens—I always hated

Dickens, because the children in his stories were so abused. I only read his novels that were class assignments, and all the time I was reading, I had such a miserable feeling of frustration.

"Does that story have a horse in it or a ghost in it?" Julie asks.

"There are lots of good stories that don't have horses or ghosts in them."

"When are we going to read it?"

"How about this afternoon?" Suddenly I am so tired. If there is a sandman, I think he's more like a cat burglar, creeping up behind me on dark, softly padded feet, smothering me in a blanket of exhaustion so heavy my head can hardly support the weight. My arms and legs feel limp, no help whatsoever. "Maybe I can take a nap first," I add.

"All right," she says. "First you sleep." She looks pleased. I guess she likes the idea of being read to after all.

How am I going to make that phone call? Julie will hear me. Mrs. Cardenas will hear me. There has to be some way. But what is it?

Mrs. Cardenas comes in carrying her handbag. "Angie is always late, too. Drives like that and still is late."

I climb to my feet. "I'm going to read *Tom Sawyer* to Julie.

"¡*Muy bien!* There's a nice breeze right now. You might like to sit on the porch while you read."

She's given me a terrific idea. "Why don't we

go out there now while we wait for your sister-in-law?"

"It's a little warm out there for me," she says. Then she chuckles. "But think how Angie will feel when she comes and we're all out there waiting for her. I hope she'll feel guilty about being late."

She and I settle into the webbed chairs. Julie sits on the steps. It's hard to sit still. The lake is silvery gray in the sun, and heat shimmers up from the street. I lift my face to the breeze that riffles across the porch.

"We're going to have a hot summer," Mrs. Cardenas says. She fans herself with her handbag. "Clouds are building up over to the west. Maybe we'll have rain. We need it."

"Excuse me for a moment. I'll be right back." I get up slowly, hoping my plan will work, hoping I'll have enough time. Julie stays where she is. Mrs. Cardenas keeps fanning.

Into the house, quickly, quickly. The phone is in their bedroom. The strange feeling of another person's room, the fragrance of the two people who have lived here for many years, making this their own domain. I feel like a trespasser. The number is clear in my mind, but the phone dial is so slow. The operator at the hospital answers.

"Dr. Lynn Manning, please."

"Can you speak up? I can't hear you."

"Dr. Lynn Manning." I clear my throat.

"One moment." Two moments. Three moments. Hurry!

Finally a voice answers, but it's not Dr. Lynn.

"This is Dina Harrington. May I please speak to Dr. Manning?"

"Hi, Dina. This is Alice. How are you feeling?"

"Fine. I'm fine. I—oh, could I speak to Dr. Manning?"

"Gee, I'm sorry," Alice says. "She's at some meetings today. I think she's coming back this evening. Do you want to leave a message?"

Now what do I do? If she calls back, I can't talk to her. Someone else will be around. I'll have to think of a better plan. This one isn't working.

"Dina? Are you there?"

"I was trying to think. No, I won't leave a message. I'll just call back tomorrow maybe."

"Okay. I'm glad it wasn't anything important. Take care."

I replace the receiver on its cradle and walk back into the hallway. Julie is standing in the living room, watching me. Do I look as guilty as I feel? I hope not.

"What were you doing in Mrs. Cardenas's bedroom?" she demands.

"I was on the phone. Didn't you hear me talking?"

"No. I just came inside. Mrs. Cardenas left. I didn't hear the phone ring, either."

"I doubt if you can hear the phone ring when you're out on the porch." I hope to distract her.

"Weren't you going to show me some other things in your box?"

"It's not time yet."

"All right. Whenever you want."

"Are you going to take your nap now?"

"I'd better stay with you."

"I'm going to watch television. You could watch it with me."

I nod.

"You could sleep in the big chair, like Mr. Cardenas does." She pauses. "Those big chairs aren't very comfortable, though."

"It's all right."

"If you want to sleep in your bed, you could. I'll be right here in the living room, watching the television. If you need me, you can call me, and I'll hear you."

She seems so eager to please, and the idea of stretching out on the bed is so tempting. There should be no problems.

Julie follows me into the bedroom. "Do you think Mrs. Cardenas would care if we turned off the air conditioner in here for a little while? Then you won't feel so cold."

"I don't think she'd mind, unless it put a strain on the others in the house." I move away from the blasts of chilly air coming from the window unit.

"We can shut the door," Julie answers, and quickly turns the dial on the air conditioner to the off position. The motor grinds and sputters to a halt. The silence is a blessing.

"What a good idea, Julie!" I smile at her, and she smiles back.

It's funny how sometimes you can be so tired you go past the need to sleep, like a clock that's been wound so tightly the mainspring twangs loose. I lie on the bed in the quietness of the room, staring at the little bumps and marks in the plaster on the ceiling. If I talk to Dr. Lynn—*when* I talk to Dr. Lynn. What do I say? I have to think it out, so there will be no time wasted. The accident. The near accident. The man Julie saw. The glass duck she destroyed. The apartment. Her treasure box.

Her treasure box.

I'm not a snoop. At the same time I tell myself that this is an emergency situation. There may be something in that box that gives the answers. Should I ask her to show me the contents? She won't do it. She was very careful to let me see only the picture of her father. She said there was more to show me, but it wasn't the right time. Suppose I ask her if now is the time?

Suppose I find the treasure box and look for myself?

Off the bed. Barefoot, and the braided rug is stiff under my toes. Where would she put it, and why do I feel so guilty?

I check the chest of drawers first. Quiet. Not a sound. Slowly. Carefully. Ease it open. Feel around through her things.

Nothing in any of the drawers. No point in checking my own. What about the closet? It must be in the closet. Wait—under the bed. The braided rug scratches my cheek. Nothing there. Too obvious. I should have known.

There isn't much in the closet. How could she have hidden it? It couldn't be in this room. It's not behind the guitar. Where is the box?

As I back out of the closet, I realize something isn't right. There's a strange smell. Gas!

I open the door. Tendrils of the invisible odor creep through the hallway. Run! Don't breathe! Throw open the front door! Wide! And the kitchen door! It's the oven! It's on and wide open! I turn it off and scream, "Julie! Where are you?"

She's in one of the plush chairs, staring at me. "Julie! Get out of here!"

I pull at her arm, and she stirs. We choke and cough as I drag her out of the house, down the porch steps, and onto the lawn. Thank God for the breeze! It's much stronger, scudding blue-black clouds ahead of it.

"What do you think you were doing?" I shout at Julie.

"I was making some lunch for us."

"With the gas on full, coming out of the open oven?"

Her lip curls out again in a gesture that's familiar to me now. "I put some cheese slices on the bread, and put them on the broiler. Then turned the oven on to broil. That's all."

There is the drip, drip of the air conditioner in the living room window. The drops slap the wooden porch. "You turned off the air conditioner in the living room, Julie. Did you turn off the one in Mrs. Cardenas's bedroom, too?"

The wind pushes in sudden spurts against my back. It carries the sharp fragrance of rain.

"I liked the quiet," Julie says. "It was nice in our bedroom with the air conditioner off, and I wasn't hot. Air conditioners in windows make a lot of noise."

"Julie, have you ever turned on an oven before?"

"Of course. Lots of times. Sometimes when no one came home, I made bread and cheese for myself. All you do is just turn them on."

"You must have used ovens with automatic pilots or electric ovens. Didn't you smell the gas?"

"Something smelled funny, but I didn't know what it was."

How can she look so innocent? She must be innocent. Surely she wouldn't— "Don't you know you could have killed us?"

She opens her mouth wide and wails, and I find myself hushing her, comforting her. "I know you wouldn't do it on purpose, Julie. I know."

The wind taps my back with a low bough from the crape myrtle. "I'll open most of the windows. This wind will help clear the air. You sit here on the porch. Right here. Okay?"

"Okay," Julie repeats. She huddles on the top step. I enter the house, throwing open all the windows except those with air conditioners attached.

Having both doors wide has already helped, and the wind is a bonus.

The house comes to life. The curtains rise and quiver. Papers from the living room table ruffle to the floor. The nearly empty napkin holder is knocked off the kitchen table with a clatter. I stand in the doorway, staring at the oven. There is the open broiler with two slices of cheese-covered bread. Julie was telling the truth.

Julie, who was sitting in the doily-draped chair, eyes staring as I ran into the room.

I lean against the wall, cold to the bone. Cold bones. Cold body. Cold mind. The cheese and bread are props. If Julie had thought they were broiling, she'd be in the kitchen watching them, wouldn't she? Cheese melts and browns in a hurry, burns in that extra instant.

I've been asking questions and avoiding the answers. Face it. I've looked at the scars on Julie's body, heard about the scars on Julie's life, and told myself, poor Julie, poor Julie, there is nothing wrong with Julie's mind.

Now I'm frightened. Should I tell Mrs. Cardenas what I think? No. She wouldn't understand this any more than I do. I've got to talk to Dr. Lynn. But what should I say? Are my suspicions enough?

"Can I come in now? It's starting to rain." Pitiful little voice, begging to be forgiven.

"Then we'd better get these windows down,"

I say. "You can help me." I hurry to each room, yanking sashes in place and fastening them. Julie works with me, a helpful nine-year-old. We leave open gaps in two of the porch windows and the window over the kitchen sink to suck in the coolness of the rain-washed air.

The red plush lion's mouth is scratchy-soft, and I drop into it, stretching my legs and curling my toes. Julie comes to stand in front of me.

"I'm hungry, Dina. I want some lunch. Will you teach me how to make the oven work?"

"Let's try some of Carmen's *empanadas* instead," I tell her. "I don't smell any more gas in the house, but I'd rather wait awhile to light the oven."

Now is the time. There are some answers I need, and I want them before I talk to Dr. Lynn. "Julie, why don't you bring me your treasure box? You said there were some things in it that you wanted to show me. I'd like to see them, and we can talk about them."

"I'm hungry," Julie says. And in the same matter-of-fact voice she adds, "My box is in another secret place. Even if you look and look, you'll never be able to find it."

CHAPTER
12

The rain is a squall that pounds and passes. Mrs. Cardenas comes home after it has gone. "We sat it out in the parking lot," she says. "I had to hear all about the problems Angie's daughter Nina is having with her husband. It wouldn't be so bad, except everybody knows the story, and I heard it first from Carmen."

Blue slips into sharp little corners. Watching me slantwise, watching and waiting.

"Did everything go all right today? Well, it must have. I see you turned off the air conditioners when it cooled down. Good for you. Did you have enough for lunch? I forgot to tell you, there's some chocolate ice cream in the freezer section."

She has answered her own question, but I feel I must say something. "We had a little trouble with the oven," I tell her. "The pilot light wasn't on, so there was gas in the house. We opened all the windows and aired it out." I wish I knew more about psychology. Right now I think Julie needs stability, and Dr. Lynn would know how to help her, not Mrs. Cardenas. My suspicions would only frighten Mrs. Cardenas.

"*¡Por supuesto!* I should have shown you how to light the pilot," she says. She begins to unbutton her blouse as she moves toward the hallway. "Let me change clothes, and we'll get dinner started. Who wants to peel potatoes?"

"I do," I answer.

Julie says, "I'll watch."

So she wants to be near me. Good. It will help me keep watch over her.

And so it goes through the rest of the day and on into the evening. We read the first chapter of *Tom Sawyer*, and she seems interested until she notices it's time for cartoons on television, and she insists that we watch them together. She's my tagalong, and after dinner she sits on her bed and watches me brush my hair. I think it's at least half an inch longer.

I take out what is left of the tiny bottle of the perfume I got for Christmas and dab it on my neck and wrists. I don't know what good it will do. The spicy tomato-onion fragrance of the stew Mrs. Cardenas cooked for dinner has blanketed the house. It overpowers the perfume.

Mrs. Cardenas pokes her head in the doorway.

"You look very pretty in that yellow dress, Dina. We can take it in around the shoulders and back, but for now it doesn't matter. Girls look pretty in dresses. Dave will like how you look tonight."

"Dave is just a friend," I tell her.

She giggles. "Sure he is, and I hope there'll be lots of Daves in your life. *Sea lo que sea*, it's nice for a girl to have boyfriends who put pink spots in their cheeks."

She leaves to answer the telephone, but she is soon back. She looks at me questioningly. "Dr. Manning is on the phone for you, Dina. She says she's returning your call."

"Thank you," I say. I don't look at Julie.

I go into her bedroom and pick up the phone. I feel as though everyone in the house was listening.

"I got your message, Dina. Is everything all right?"

"I'm sorry to bother you. I told Alice it wasn't important. I—I just wanted to talk to you."

"How is everything going with Mrs. Cardenas?"

"Fine. She and her husband are very good to us."

"And Julie?"

Not a sound. They can hear every word I say. "How is Dr. Paull? Are you still dating him?"

She pauses. "You didn't call to ask about my personal life. Do you need to talk to me, but you can't right now?"

"Yes."

"Is it something urgent?"

"I don't know." I have to get the answers first. When I talk to Dr. Lynn about Julie, I want to be fair. I want all the facts in place, not just suspicions. I know there are too many people who come to the hospital for help, too few people to help them. Julie should have the best help possible.

"I've got a pretty heavy load for the next few days," she says. "Maybe Thursday you could call me, or try to come by the hospital. But if you need to see me before then, don't hesitate to phone. Will that work out for you, Dina?"

"That will be fine," I answer.

As I finish the call, it's as though the house breathes again. There are footsteps in the hall, and Mrs. Cardenas is telling Julie that Carmen's children are going to come to play on Saturday.

I join them.

"Well, Dina," she says, "how was Dr. Lynn?"

"We didn't chat much. She just asked how everything was going, and I told her fine." She's looking at me intently. So is Julie. What else do I say? "She's dating Dr. Paull."

"Everybody knows that," Mrs. Cardenas says.

The ache at the back of my mind becomes words. "I wish she had told me she'd take me back to the home to visit again."

"Ahhh. That's it." Mrs. Cardenas's arm is around my shoulders. "You're homesick, *niñita*. That I can understand. But I'll try to make you a happy home here."

The doorbell rings, and she propels herself away from me and down the hall, calling, "That will be Dave."

Julie hasn't said a word. She is the little cat, staring, staring.

"Mr. and Mrs. Cardenas are kind. This will be a good place to stay," I tell her. One last sweep with the hairbrush.

"For the rest of your life," she says.

Oh, dear. I haven't time. I can hear Dave's voice and Mrs. Cardenas's treble punctuation. "Julie, I tried to explain to you about what Dave and I said. I thought you understood."

"Dina! Dave is here!"

"Julie, I have to see Dave now."

Julie, without a word, hops off the bed and walks ahead of me down the hall.

"Hi," Dave says to her. He smiles at me.

"The evening is so nice," Mrs. Cardenas says. "You young people go out on the front porch. It's too stuffy in here."

"Stuffy?" Mr. Cardenas says, peering over the top of his newspaper. "Then why don't you turn on the air conditioners again?"

"Be quiet, Carlos," she says.

Mrs. Cardenas opens the door. Dave and I go outside, Julie with us.

"Julie," Dave says, "I bet there's something you want to watch on television."

"I want to be with you and Dina," she says.

"Not this time," he says.

"Let her stay, Dave." She's so small, so much alone.

But Mrs. Cardenas has noticed Julie's absence, and the door opens. "Julie," she says, "I'm making popcorn for Carlos. Come and help me."

"Popcorn?" Mr. Cardenas says. "You know I can't eat popcorn with these teeth!"

Mrs. Cardenas has pulled Julie inside, and the door closes.

"Sit down," Dave says quietly. He pulls the two chairs together. "I thought of something."

I wish I could see his expression, but the porch is mottled in black and moonlight, and Dave's face is in darkness.

"Last year our high school put on the musical *Oliver*," he says. "You know *Oliver*, don't you?"

"I saw the movie years ago, but I hated it. I hated the way the children had to live. I never liked Dickens."

"Don't you remember? The bad guy in the story was Bill Sikes."

I gasp. "And the woman who loved him—wasn't her name—?"

We say it together. "Nancy."

"Wait a minute!" Memories are rushing back. "And she sang a song—"As Long As He Needs Me"! Oh, Dave! That's the play Julie's mother was in, and she took the part of Nancy!"

"When was this?"

"It must have been years ago. Julie says when she was little, her father took her to see the play."

"What if there was something between - her mother and the guy who played Bill Sikes? What if Julie just kept thinking of him as Sikes?"

"Her mother's name really was Nancy. That would fit." Thoughts fall into place. "No wonder the police couldn't trace Sikes. He'd have another name."

"Julie told you that he fought with her father. He must have threatened him, or Nancy. Maybe that's why they kept moving and had to move so fast."

Should I tell him the rest? It's too long, too complicated. Not now. Not until after I sort it all out. Not until after I talk to Dr. Lynn.

"I'm so glad you came up with this," I say. "I'm going to try to get Julie to open up to me tomorrow. She must know things she isn't telling. I'm hoping I can get her to confide in me."

He reaches over to take my hand, but I stand up. "Dave, she stuck to me like butter on bread today. I know she's jealous of you and the time I spend with you. Right now I've got to make her feel she's important to me."

He stands, too. "So you're telling me to go home?"

"I don't want to, but I have to."

He shrugs but doesn't let go of my hand. "There's one thing more. I went to the library this morning, and I read whatever I could find in back issues of magazines and newspapers about Hodgkin's disease and leukemia and other kinds of cancer. Do you know how much progress they're making, Dina? Do you know they're finding new things every day, that your chances keep getting better? You've got to want to fight."

"How many knights were eaten before one of them finally killed the dragon? How many—?"

But his mouth is over mine, and I respond. Until I remember that it's not fair.

"No, Dave." I tug away from him. My voice is hoarse, and I've forgotten what else I was going to say.

"Dina, don't hate yourself."

I back away, reaching for the doorknob. "But I can't help it. I do!"

There's no time for him to answer. I'm inside the door, leaning against it, trembling. I don't want to talk about it. Dave doesn't understand how I feel. I wish with all my heart that he could understand.

Mrs. Cardenas looks up from her bowl of popcorn. "Where's Dave?"

"He had to go home."

"Before he had some popcorn?"

"The whole world is not waiting for popcorn," Mr. Cardenas says, and he turns the television sound up.

"What did Dave want to talk to you about?" Julie asks.

"This is a good program," I tell her, as I sit on the floor. "If we talk, we'll spoil it."

Before I go to bed, I get out my stationery box. It's just where I had left it. I prop myself against the pillow, box on my knees, sheet of pink stationery on the box. *Dear Holley Jo.* The only words on the paper. *I met this really super guy named Dave. Tonight—*

But I don't want to tell Holley Jo about the way I feel. For a while I need to keep all this to myself. I put the box on the floor and turn out the light.

Holley Jo, Holley Jo. Once again I'll slip away and glide up the road and through the walls and into the green and yellow room. But tonight it doesn't work. Tonight, until I sleep, I hold the smell of Dave's skin and the feel of Dave's lips. Tonight I don't want to go away.

In the morning Mrs. Cardenas says, "It's a beautiful day!" She puts a bowl of cereal before me and passes me a stack of buttered slices of raisin toast.

The kitchen window is wide open. The air holds the memory of the rainstorm, and it's sharp and sweet.

"This is a good day to take a walk." I can get Julie out of the house. Get her to a place where we can talk without anyone overhearing. "Julie, we haven't walked to the lake yet. Why don't we go this morning?"

Morning is a good time to begin things, to plan

things, even to end things before the day weaves itself into a heavy mass of problems and concerns.

Julie gulps down a swallow of orange juice. "Why don't we go to the zoo?"

Her question takes me by surprise. "Because the zoo is too far away to walk."

"You promised to take me to the zoo, and you didn't."

"Dave said he'd take us, but we planned that for the future."

Julie takes a bite of toast. "I've never ridden on an elephant. More than anything in the world I want to ride on the elephant at the zoo. You said I could."

"Be reasonable. How could we get to the zoo?"

"You can drive, Dina. Mrs. Cardenas could let us use her car."

"Julie!"

But Mrs. Cardenas gives Julie a fond look. "I suppose I could do that. We have to be careful of gas, you know. It costs a lot now. But this one time. The zoo isn't far."

I wish Julie hadn't done this. "I'm sorry, Mrs. Cardenas. She shouldn't have asked. We can wait until Dave takes us."

Julie is looking at Mrs. Cardenas with eyes that are so pleading she reminds me of a miserable waif begging for pennies. I want a chance to talk to Julie, not the distractions of the zoo.

"It's okay," Mrs. Cardenas says. "I'll pack you

a picnic lunch, and give you some spending money for the zoo and the little train."

"Please don't," I tell her. "We can go another time."

"No, no. Don't worry. Now is a good time. It's going to be a nice day, not too hot, no more rain." She rinses off plates as she talks, stacking them on the drainboard. "The weatherman on TV said so, and I believe it, even though he's usually wrong. You know, Arturo's Jimmy would make a better weatherman because ever since he broke his arm in a baseball game, he can tell if it's going to rain."

She begins to putter in and out of the refrigerator, putting together a lunch for us. Julie is pleased. Well, maybe this will put her in a good mood. It might be for the best. I'll need her cooperation to get the right answers.

"If you go early, it isn't too crowded," Mrs. Cardenas says. "So finish your breakfast, then get the map, and I'll show you how to get there."

Mrs. Cardenas gives me other instructions before we leave. "Be back before three o'clock. A woman is coming here to check things out. She has some papers to sign, and she wants to talk to both of you."

"We'll be here," I tell her, and I climb behind the wheel, tucking the lunch bag on the floor next to me. Julie gets in, carefully holding a paper sack.

I'm watching streets, so it's not until we are past

McCullough that I notice the paper sack is folded and on the floor. On her lap Julie holds her treasure box.

"Oh!"

Julie stares up at me, and I say, "You brought the box. I'm glad. Are you going to show me some of the things in it?"

"Yes," she says. "Today is the time."

I lean forward, following signs. Here's a turnoff. *Zoo.* Over on the left. There we go. Up the road. "Look, Julie. Horses to ride. Did you ever ride a horse?"

"No. They're too big. I don't want to."

"Did you ever ride ponies?"

"My father took me for pony rides a lot when I was little."

She isn't very big now. She sits stiffly on the seat, clinging to her faded, dented treasure box, and I feel a pang of tenderness toward her. So many mixed-up problems. But I know Dr. Lynn will be able to help her.

Around the curve to the right. We must be entering the park from a back road. We pass the train tracks and a small train that is chugging along.

Julie stares out the window. "I want to ride on that train."

"There's lots of time. Why don't we find a nice, quiet place for a talk, and you can show me the things in your treasure box?"

"Not until after we ride on the train and the elephant."

To the left is the entrance to the zoo. I park the car. Julie slides her treasure box under the seat.

"We'll lock the car," she says. She's in charge all the way. The best thing I can do is go along with her plans.

She chooses the train first, and I buy the tickets at the little station. We sit together in a car with a pink-striped canopy top. *Plackety-plackety-plackety-plackety* over the rails, chugging and humming to the next station. Around the park. There are the horses again.

"Look, Julie! A squirrel!" Back to the station. Around in a circle. I wish Dave were with us.

We walk up the incline to the zoo, pay our admission, and go inside. There is so much to see.

"Find out where the elephants are," Julie says. "I want to go right to the elephants."

It's her zoo, her show. Why did it have to be today? What's on her mind? I can't even guess.

There is the elephant with a platform of sorts on his back, and there is the line for the ride. I buy Julie a ticket, and she has already claimed her place in line.

"That looks like fun," I tell her.

"I've never ridden an elephant," she says so solemnly that it's hard to keep from smiling.

Finally it's her turn, and she climbs up to join the other children in the carrier strapped to the elephant's back. She twists to look at me, and I smile and wave at her. She waves once, then turns to face forward. The elephant begins to move.

It's a short trip around the compound. Her group climbs off as another group climbs on. Most of the children run to their mothers, but Julie walks to me, still solemn, something very much on her mind.

"Now let's have lunch," she says.

"But you haven't seen the rest of the zoo."

"I rode on the elephant. That's all I wanted to do."

"Are you sure? Because once we go out, we can't go in without paying again."

"Come on, Dina," she says, taking my hand and leading me back the way we had come.

Picnic tables are scattered among the oak trees near the parking lot. I carry the lunch from the car and spread it out on a table deep in shade. Julie carries her treasure box.

Sandwiches, bananas, apples, and oatmeal cookies. How does Mrs. Cardenas expect us to eat all this!

There's a Thermos of lemonade and some paper cups. I pour the lemonade and put a cup before Julie, who climbs on the bench next to me. She munches on a cookie and gulps the lemonade.

"Maybe it's too early," I tell her. "I'm just not hungry. I'd rather talk."

"All right," Julie says. She moves her empty cup aside and puts the treasure box in its place. She struggles for a moment with the metal lid, then pulls it off. This time she places the lid to one side.

There are not many things in the box. There is a small doll, some seashells, a picture postcard of

Sarasota, and another with a scene of sand dunes spiked with sea grass.

Julie holds up an inexpensive gilded chain. "See, I told you I had a gold chain," she says. "My father gave it to me."

"I remember. You said you could put your jade ring on it." Her fingers are bare. "Julie, what happened to the ring?"

She doesn't look at me. "I lost it."

The pink glass dog is in the box, but she moves it aside and takes out a newspaper clipping from a Tulsa paper. It's a picture of a pretty brunette woman dressed in a ragged costume. A man is standing beside her, but the paper has been torn on a diagonal, so his face is gone.

"That's when my mother was in the play *Oliver*," Julie says.

"She's beautiful." I read the caption: Nancy Gambrell as Nancy and William Kaines as Bill Sikes.

"Julie!" I'm confused. "This says that William Kaines— But I thought your father's name was William Kaines!"

"No. That's not my father's name."

"Your name is Julie Kaines."

"It's not. It's Julie Gambrell."

"But in the hospital they called you Julie Kaines."

For a moment she looks bewildered. "No, they didn't. They just called me Julie. That's all."

I stare at her. "They took it for granted. No one ever asked you your last name!"

A serrated leaf spirals down on the paper, and I brush it away. "Then the man in the car wasn't your father."

"Of course not," she says.

I examine the yellowed clipping in my hands. "Julie, why is the photograph in the newspaper torn?"

"I tore off his head," she says. "I hate Bill Sikes."

CHAPTER 13

"I think we'd better talk about Sikes," I say slowly.

"You haven't seen everything in the box yet," she answers. She pushes it toward me. Again she calmly takes command.

There are two more snapshots, with a background of trees and a pond. The figures are small. A young man and a young woman. The man is holding a very young child with windblown silver for hair. Julie hands them to me.

"This is you with your parents?"

Julie nods.

Again I look at the photo of her father. "You look so much like him. What was his name?"

"Gordon Peter Gambrell."

"Tell me more about your parents. Tell me about your mother."

But Julie doubles over and holds her stomach. "I feel sick, Dina."

"It must be the lemonade and cookie. Too much sugar. I should have made sure you ate a sandwich first."

"No. I felt sick before I ate."

"You didn't say anything about it."

"I thought it would go away."

"I'll take you home right now." I'm up and packing the lunch back in the bag.

Julie curls into a little ball and moans.

"Do you want to go to the restroom?"

"I want to go to the hospital."

"But Julie—"

It occurs to me that might be a good idea. If I took her home, Mrs. Cardenas would have to call the doctor, and we'd probably end up taking Julie to see him. This way she can be checked immediately, and if it is serious, she'll have good care. And I can try to talk to Dr. Lynn. It's more important now than ever that I talk to Dr. Lynn.

Julie must be feeling terrible. She doesn't seem to care about her treasure box. I pack her things in carefully and snap the lid shut. "If you can stand up, I'll try to carry you."

"I can walk. Just help me."

We struggle up the slight hill. My arms are filled with the bag of food, the treasure box, and Julie. "Here's the car. Just a minute. I'll get the door open."

She leans heavily against me, and I nearly fall. "I want to lie down in the backseat," she says.

"I'd feel better about it if you were in the front seat with me. You can put your head on my lap."

"No."

"Please, Julie. Get in the front seat."

"I'll get sick. It would be all over you."

As though she's proving her point, she retches. The important thing is to get Julie to the hospital, so I open the back door.

"Here you go. Can you manage to get in? Let me help."

She lies on the seat, curling into a ball, knees almost to her chin, her eyes squeezed shut. "Hurry up, Dina," she says.

I scramble into the driver's seat, drop the keys, fumble them into the ignition, and guide the car from the parking lot. How do we get out of the park? There's a sign—Broadway. I know that will take me to Hildebrand.

As we pull onto Broadway, she says, "You have to go on the freeway to get to the hospital, don't you?"

"Yes." I try to see her in the rearview mirror, but she's too low. "Will that bother you?"

"It's faster. I want you to drive fast."

"I'll do the best I can. Are you in pain?"

She doesn't answer, just makes little mewling noises. At the stoplight I check the map again to get my bearings. Hildebrand to I-10. "Okay, Julie,"

I say, trying to sound confident, "we'll be on the freeway in a few minutes. And then it's not far to the hospital."

There's not much traffic on I-10 this time of day, and it's moving at a fairly fast clip. I try to keep my speed around sixty, but I'm nervous. Each time Julie gives a little moan, my foot becomes heavier on the accelerator.

I swing around a pickup truck, pulling into the right lane ahead of him, and realize I'm going much too fast, so I pull it down to sixty again.

There's a movement in my rearview mirror, and I look into it, startled. Julie looks back at me. She's sitting right behind me, leaning on the back of my seat.

"Are you feeling better?" I ask her.

"I have to tell you something," she says.

"Sure, Julie. What is it?"

"I hated Sikes because he killed my father and ran away, taking my mother and me with him. And I hated him more when he hurt me. And I hated Nancy because she didn't stop him."

"Oh, Julie."

"You said you would stay with me, Dina. You promised. And then I found out that you didn't mean it, that you're going to die and leave me all alone. So I hate you, too."

"Listen, Julie. It's not like that. I—"

"When the car crashed, we were all supposed to die—Sikes and Nancy and me. Sikes is angry because I didn't."

"Julie, let's talk to Dr. Lynn. She can help you."

"Do you know how I did it? I put my arm around Sikes's neck—like this!"

My head is jerked back. There's a steel vise around my windpipe. I can't breathe! I can't see!

I slam on the brakes, and Julie flies forward against me, breaking her grip. There is a loud screech of tires behind us. I grapple with Julie, pulling her into the front seat. And at the same time I brace myself, waiting for the crash.

But instead, the door on Julie's side is flung open, and someone dives into the car. He grabs Julie, trying to pull her away from me. "Put on your brake!" he yells.

I manage to get the car into park and yank the keys from the ignition. For a few moments we are a tangle of struggling bodies in the front seat. When I can manage to look up, still gasping for breath, he is on his knees, wedged between the dashboard and the front seat, pinning Julie down.

He's a fairly young man, black felt western hat shoved to the back of his head. "I saw what happened from my pickup," he says. "Then your car went all over the road. Sure give you credit for smarts, girl. Or else dumb luck. Now we got to get us off this damn freeway."

An eighteen-wheeler pulls up in front of us. The driver comes back to check, then runs to his truck and radios for help. It doesn't take long for a police car to arrive.

"She needs a doctor," I tell them. "Oh, please

help her." And I give the nearest policeman some of Julie's background information. "Detective Mac-Garvey will know all about it."

Julie doesn't cry. She doesn't make a sound. She just stares at me.

"Don't hate me, Julie," I tell her. "Look—I'll take care of your treasure box for you. I'll put it in the closet at Mrs. Cardenas's house and keep it for you until you want it again."

But she doesn't answer.

It's an hour and many questions later when Dr. Lynn and Dr. Paull come together into the small brown office where I've been waiting. I'm so glad to see them that I lean against Dr. Lynn, holding her tightly. MacGarvey has called and given them most of the story.

"After all that you drove here to the police station by yourself?" Dr. Paull asks.

"I followed the police car." It's funny, but I can't remember much about it. I wonder what happened to the man in the pickup truck. The policemen must have his name.

"I'll have to call Mrs. Cardenas," I add.

"Detective MacGarvey did that for you."

Detective MacGarvey comes into the room. "Now we're getting somewhere," he says. "I've been matching descriptions given by robbery victims in a number of nearby states, and they seem to add up to William Kaines. It looks like he committed a couple of robberies here in the city a week before he died in that car crash."

"Did you find out if he murdered Julie's father?"

"She had that story wrong," he says. "Maybe her mother told her that her father was dead. Maybe she jumped to the wrong conclusion. About three years ago a Gordon P. Gambrell was taken to a hospital in Tulsa, Oklahoma, pretty badly beaten after a fight."

"She said Sikes fought with her father!" I interrupt.

"When Gambrell got out of the hospital, his family was gone. There was something put out on his wife and child, but that information wasn't on the computer printout I got on Kaines last week."

"Can you call her father? Tell him about Julie?"

He nods. "It might take a day or two to track him down, but we'll let him know Julie is here in San Antonio."

The question I've been so afraid to ask: "They won't arrest her for murder, will they?"

Dr. Lynn puts an arm tightly around my shoulders. "Julie will get the help she needs. Isn't that right, Mr. MacGarvey?"

"It'll come down to that," he says. He gives me a pat on the shoulder. "If you want to go home now, you can." He shakes hands with Dr. Paull and strides from the room.

"Can we sit here for just a few minutes?" I ask them. "I'm still shaking inside."

"Of course," Dr. Lynn says. "Julie's doctor is with her now. It will be a little while before they'll let me talk to her."

We settle on the bench, one of them on each side of me.

"There's something else I have to tell you," I say.

"About Julie?"

"About me. I was fighting for my life."

"We heard about that," Dr. Paull says. "It must have been a terrifying experience."

"You aren't listening to what I'm saying," I tell him. "I was fighting to stay alive. When it came right down to it, I must have wanted to live."

Dr. Lynn grips my hand tightly.

"I've decided to work at those odds," I say. "I suppose I've been doing it all along, but I couldn't see beyond the anger."

"Good for you," Dr. Paull says. Then he gives kind of a scratchy little cough and takes my other hand.

Dr. Lynn smiles at me. "Why don't we drive up next weekend so you can give this news to your friend Holley Jo?" she asks.

"I'd love to," I answer. "And can I bring someone with me? His name is Dave."

ABOUT THE AUTHOR

Joan Lowery Nixon is the author of over forty books for young readers, including *The Kidnapping of Christina Lattimore* and *The Séance*, both of which won the Edgar Award for the best juvenile mystery of the year, and both available in Dell Laurel-Leaf editions. She and her husband, Hershell Nixon, have published four books on nature and energy. They live in Houston and have four grown children.

F
Nix   Nixon, Joan Lowery
         The Specter

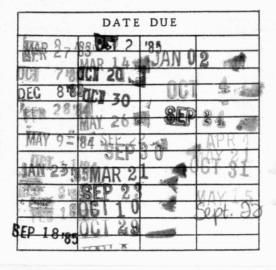

DATE DUE			
MAR 27 '83	OCT 2 '85		
APR 27 '83	MAR 14	JAN 02	
OCT 7 '83	OCT 20		
DEC 8 '83	OCT 30	OCT 4	
FEB 28 '84	MAY 26	SEP 24	
MAY 9 '84	SEP	APR 4	
JAN 23 '85	SEP 30	MAY 21	
	MAR 21	OCT 31	
DEC 6	SEP 23	MAY 15	
NOV 18	OCT 10	Sept. 23	
SEP 18 '85	OCT 29		

137   83

MEDIALOG
Alexandria, Ky 41001